Born in 1948, Ernesto Mallo is a published essayist,
newspaper columnist, screenwriter and playwright.
He is a former anti-Junta activist who was pursued
by the dictatorship. *Needle in a Haystack* is his first
novel and the first in a trilogy with superintendent
Lascano. The first two are being made into films in
Argentina.

NEEDLE IN A HAYSTACK

Ernesto Mallo

Translated by Jethro Soutar

BITTER LEMON PRESS
LONDON

BITTER LEMON PRESS

First published in the United Kingdom in 2010 by
Bitter Lemon Press, 37 Arundel Gardens, London W11 2LW

www.bitterlemonpress.com

First published in Spanish as *La aguja en el pajar*
by Grupo Editorial Planeta, Buenos Aires, 2006

Bitter Lemon Press gratefully acknowledges the financial
assistance of the Arts Council of England

Work published within the framework of "Sur" Translation Support
Program of the Ministry of Foreign Affairs, International Trade
and Worship of the Argentine Republic

A CIP record for this book is available from the British Library
ISBN 978–1–904738–56–5

Typeset by Alma Books Ltd
Printed and bound by Cox & Wyman Ltd, Reading, Berkshire

Tomorrow or the day after, catastrophe will come, drowning us all in blood, if we haven't already been reduced to ashes. Everyone is scared. Me included; I can't sleep at night, overcome with terror, nothing functions, all we have is our fear... So what does Superintendent Bauer do? He does his job, tries to create a little order and sense where there is only chaos and irreversible disintegration. But he's not alone...

Ingmar Bergman
The Serpent's Egg

1

*I know that one must kill, yes
but kill who...*
Homero Expósito, 1976

Some days the side of the bed is like the edge of an enormous abyss. Day in, day out, doing things you don't want to do. Lascano wants to stay in bed for ever or throw himself into the abyss. If only the abyss were real. But it's not. Only the pain is real.

Lascano wakes up feeling like this today, and has done every day since his wife's death. Orphaned as a child, he seemed predestined to solitude. Life granted him an eight-year respite in the form of Marisa, a reason to go on living, a fleeting joy that ended less than a year ago, and left him stranded again in the shallows of an island where he earned his nickname: Perro; the Dog.

He launches himself into the void. The shower washes away the last remains of sleep, which howl as they disappear down the plughole. He gets dressed, puts his Bersa Thunder nine millimetre into its holster. Lascano goes over to the birdcage, home of the only living reminder of Marisa, and adds a pinch of seed to the feeder. He heads out into the deserted early morning. Day has yet to break. The air is so humid that Perro feels he could swim to the garage. Fog envelops everything, playing tricks with lights and shadows. He sparks up his first cigarette of the day.

As he sets off, a military operation plays out on the corner. Two olive-green Bedford trucks block off the street. Soldiers with machine guns and Fal rifles. A bus with its doors open. Passengers are lined up along one side, their backs to the soldiers, hands on heads, waiting in silence for their turn to be frisked and interrogated by a lieutenant with the face of a cruel child.

Lascano passes them with indifference. A soldier looks at Lascano, turns to his lieutenant, as though seeking an instruction, then looks at Lascano again. Lascano stares back at him with a commanding glare, making full eye contact, and the soldier lowers his gaze. Slowly, dawn breaks.

As Lascano gets to the garage, a convoy of military trucks passes by. The first one carries a boy and a girl. She wears a flowery dress and must be the same age as Marisa was when he first met her. The girl throws Lascano a fleeting look of desperation, which sends a jolt up his spine like some torturous electric shock, and then she is swallowed up by the fog. Lascano enters the black mouth of the garage. The day begins.

Walking up the ramp reminds him, one by one, of all the cigarettes he has ever smoked. While the Ford Falcon warms up, he lights his second cigarette of the day and reaches for the radio transmitter.

Fifteen to base. Over. Bow-wow. Over. Quite the joker this morning, I see. Over. If you'd spent the whole night here, you'd be in a funny mood too, Perro. Over. What you got? Over. You're to head over to the Riachuelo river. Over. Where? Over. Avenida 27 de Febrero, opposite the lake at the racetrack. Over. And? Over. Investigate a report of two bodies dumped by the hard shoulder, on the riverside. Over. Won't they be military hits? Over. I don't know, go and find out. Over. I'm on my way. Over and out.

First gear always crunches as he sets off, and does so more each time.

One of these days I'll have to get the clutch fixed on this thing before it leaves me screwed in the middle of nowhere.

The call has put him in a bad mood.

To his left, a chemical smog rises from the Riachuelo waters, poisoning the atmosphere. Lascano drives with the window open as if wanting to punish himself with the river's stench. Through the windscreen, the landscape blurs and reappears to the rhythm of the wipers. The radio is silent, the street deserted and the tyres, rolling across the tarmac, produce the monotonous *tac tac* of a train. Movement up ahead breaks his hypnosis. A Falcon Rural estate backs out of a track on the left. It has a dent in its rear door and the plastic cover on the right brake light is broken, so giving off white light instead of red. Lascano takes his foot off the accelerator, but the Rural pulls forward and tears away. Lascano gets to the track, which leads through muddy grass to a corrugated iron hut. He drives down it a few feet and makes out some shapes on the ground. He pulls to a halt, puts on the handbrake, gets out and sees the shapes for what they are: three dead bodies. He lights his third cigarette and approaches. Two of the bodies are wet with dew. Their features have been obliterated by countless bullets, their skulls destroyed. Lascano holds back a retch. He can tell that one is a girl, one a boy, and both are wearing jeans and polo necks. The third body is that of a tall man, around sixty, hefty, pot-bellied, thinning grey hair, dressed in a black suit and tie. He is bone dry and his head is intact, the wild scream of death frozen across his face. He wears no belt and at the top of his stomach a big bloodstain paints a flower on his light-blue shirt. Lascano

9

spots a piece of red plastic lying close by. He picks it up and puts it in his pocket. He lights a fourth cigarette and slowly walks back to his car. On the way, he retrieves a belt, which doubtless belonged to the dead man. The buckle is broken. He coils it up in his hand, then, back at the car, he sits down sideways in the driver's seat, with his feet out the door. He picks up the microphone.

Fifteen to base. Over. You there already? Over. How many stiffs, did you say? Over. Two. Over. Send me the ambulance, I'm moving them to Viamonte. Over. On its way. Over. I'll wait for it. Over and out.

Lascano swivels in the seat, shuts the door, finishes his cigarette and throws the stub out the window. It has started to rain. He sits up straight, takes the wheel, sets the motor running and reverses up to the main road to make himself visible for the ambulance. He waits. A refrigerator lorry goes past. One of Fuseli's old phrases comes to mind:

You never get over the death of a child; it's something you just have to live with for ever.

Fuseli knew from experience what he was talking about. Lascano was particularly struck by this comment, because Fuseli had taken good care not to reveal to Lascano that Marisa had been two-months pregnant when she died. It was the last time either of them mentioned dead children. Fuseli knew that the scar was there, but he felt no need to lick his wounds. Both he and Lascano believe men should suffer in silence. Lascano had known Fuseli for years, but until Marisa's death they had never talked of anything other than work. Fuseli is a forensic doctor, one of those people truly passionate about their job. He is short, a little fat and squat, his hair clipped, combed and gelled, face clean-shaven; everything suggests a very formal man.

But when it comes to discovering a corpse's secrets, Fuseli turns into a serious obsessive. He reaches out to the dead and they respond. Nobody has an eye for tiny details like Fuseli and nobody has his patience for spending a whole night disembowelling a body. But on the day of Marisa's funeral, Fuseli dropped everything and accompanied Lascano to La Tablada, the Jewish cemetery.

The ambulance's lights start to flash in the distance.

At the time, Perro was too broken to be surprised and he accepted Fuseli's warm embrace and his few carefully chosen words like manna from heaven. They had been friends ever since, never judging one another, never competing. Not then, in desperate times, nor in their rare moments of happiness. They were also united in using fierce concentration at work as a placebo, although they didn't talk much about this either, of course. Perhaps true friendship is better expressed by what's not said than by what is.

When the ambulance arrives, Lascano signals the way. He follows slowly behind, then tells the driver and paramedic to start loading up the bodies. Lascano inspects the fat corpse again. He checks its pockets and finds only a few coins along with a business card for the Fortuna Sawmill, with an address in Benavídez, near Tigre. He moves out of the way and watches them put the body on a stretcher.

Lascano gets back into his car, sets off and is soon behind the ambulance.

KEEP YOUR DISTANCE.

There is little traffic at this hour, and a few minutes later they pull into the yard at the mortuary. While the stretcher-bearers move the bodies, Lascano heads off to the operations room in search of his friend Fuseli. Fully concentrated at his microscope, the doctor doesn't notice Lascano's entrance.

Fuseli, this is no time to be going around so distracted. Remember what happened to Archimedes. Perro! What are you doing here? I've brought you some presents, so you don't get bored. What have you got for me?

The stretcher-bearers deposit the bodies on the dissection tables and leave. Lascano lights a cigarette. Fuseli carefully observes the three bodies and moves over to the fat man.

You got your Polaroid? Over there, in the cabinet.

Lascano goes over to the cupboard and takes out the camera, while Fuseli closely examines the corpse.

Is it loaded? It should be. The two kids were executed, but this one's different. I thought so too. Hello big guy. Are you going to tell me your secrets?

Fuseli grips the body's head and holds it up while Lascano lines up the camera and presses the red button. The machine hums, then spits out an image not yet ready to reveal itself. Lascano wafts it about in the air.

You get crazier by the day. Even a no-mark criminal knows dead men can't talk. That's because criminals are so ignorant. The dead talk to those who know how to listen to them. Anyway, people talk to plants, don't they? Does this contraption work or what? There's nothing coming out. Try it again.

Fuseli holds up the head once more. Lascano takes another photo.

What do you reckon?

Fuseli carefully examines the corpse's hands.

This one put up a fight. Do you think he was planted there? What does it look like to you? Like it couldn't be clearer if they'd left a trowel and a watering can. *The ones who are executed always show up with their faces destroyed. The old boy's is intact. Apart from these wounds. But I get the feeling he got them when he was already dead.*

Lascano looks at the photo. As if returning from beyond the grave, the dead man starts to show himself.

I would say that they killed this one somewhere else. What else would you say? Come back tomorrow and I'll tell you. Done. Hey, why don't you bring me a little weed from your pals in the drug squad? You still smoking spliff? You should be ashamed of yourself, you old hippy. I am, but then I smoke a joint and the shame passes. I'll see what I can lay my hands on. My mind thanks you in advance. Now let's see fella, where did they stick it to you?... mmm, here's the little hole where death entered and life departed...

Fuseli goes into a trance, the rest of the world disappearing as he becomes totally immersed in his work and his intimate relationship with the dead. Lascano quietly leaves the room. A light but persistent wind has cleared the sky and a sullen winter sun pokes out between the clouds. *A promising morning,* thinks Lascano, as he sits at his wheel, waiting at the mortuary gate for a fellow driver to let him into the passing traffic.

2

The room is in semi-darkness. What little light there is comes from the street lamp outside. Jolted by the wind, its faint glow dances around and throws Amancio's shadow alternately onto the ceiling, the walls and the bookcase. Sitting beside the window, he drinks his fifth whisky. He'd rather be having a Ballantine or Johnny Walker Black Label, but he has to make do with an Old Smuggler because Amancio is no longer what he once was, or at least no longer has what he once had, which amounts to the same thing in the end. And so he drinks begrudgingly.

It's past two in the morning and Lara went to sleep three hours ago. This did bring some relief, a respite from her continual reproaches, but it was also an affront to his expectations of companionship, of mutual understanding, of support, bah, of sex. But Lara is conditioned only to make demands; unless she gets something in return, she has nothing to give.

In the street below, the army has just set up one of its checkpoints. A jeep blocks the entrance to the street. Two soldiers with machine guns are positioned on each corner in the shadows. Three others have placed themselves a few feet further back and three more stop any car that happens by. The soldiers search the vehicle thoroughly, demand to see the identification papers of any passengers, split them up and bombard them with questions. The officers hunt for inconsistencies in their stories, for firearms, documents, evidence of something, whatever. The slightest grounds for suspicion means being thrown in the back of a van and driven to one of many clandestine military prisons spread across the city, to undergo a deeper, more pressing interrogation. Amancio catches himself wanting to witness an arrest. He feels like a circus-goer hoping to see the tightrope-walker fall. Time passes by, but nothing else does, the streets are empty, the soldiers, trained for action, grow bored and distracted, until at last the approach of a car brings them to attention. They aim their guns at the heads of the civilians in a car, their trigger fingers twitching as they feel their own fear levels rise, fear being the food that nourishes the soldier.

Amancio finishes his drink in one violent gulp, throwing it down his throat as if wanting to hurt himself with this harsh liquor that his palate is growing accustomed to, and serves himself another.

Somewhat drunk, he inspects his hunting trophies and framed photos. His successful past now seems strange to him. There he is, proudly brandishing his rifle, its butt resting on his thigh, his foot on the horns of a tremendous cape buffalo. He used to love the feeling of power he got from killing these enormous beasts. At his side, his friend Martinez de Hoz. Crouched down, the guide, a little black guy, all eyes and teeth. Amancio is an excellent marksman; it's his most notable skill, quite possibly his only skill. He feels nostalgic for the days of playing the white hunter, when he could happily blow a

16

fortune on an African safari in the Okavango delta, for the lost splendour and indulgence of it all, because for some time now Amancio's finances have been spiralling out of control. He was never taught nor felt the need to learn how to earn money, only to spend it. He was an awful student guided by an indifferent father, from whom Amancio inherited the sense of a life already accounted for, nails growing long like those of a Chinese mandarin. Work was not meant for the likes of them. Their distant ancestors had made fortunes appropriating Indian land in the wake of the desert campaign of General Roca. Back then, just as today, the army lived by a non-negotiable principle: that the good fight meant fighting for goods. The sacrifice, the massacre of one thousand Indians per day, wasn't considered excessive in return for securing a family's wealth for three or four generations. Amancio's grandfather had been the sort who took his family to Europe for long holidays, travelling with his own cow on board the ship to provide fresh milk for his children, and a lover among the passengers on the lower deck to fulfil those functions that bored his aristocratic wife, who considered sex to be something for the working classes. In the salons of Paris they coined the phrase "as rich as an Argentine". A plentiful childhood, summers spent on the estate at Rauch: twenty thousand acres of the best land in the country. Hereditary tradition ensured that money fell from heaven at the same rate that relatives rose up to it. Life revolved around travel, impressing one's contemporaries in the salons, swanning around with beautiful, languid young women, gossiping about the "parvenus" and the fallen, mocking the nouveaux riches, scorning the poor, scoffing at the latest scandals and enjoying oneself in the eccentric company of

17

aristocrats, the Beccar Varelas and the Pereyra Iraolas of this world.

But inheritances were divided among all heirs and a lack of occupation eventually proved costly, especially to someone accustomed to an expensive lifestyle and the finest imported luxuries, unable to renounce old ways, to make a living for himself. Hardly anything was left of all that grandeur today. Of what had once been a vast estate, there's now only La Rencorosa ranch: a few gardens and flowers, two-hundred-year-old trees, the Sudan grass, the barn where a pair of old nags sleep, half a dozen chickens that survive the neglect of their master and a disused tractor. The big ochre house, spacious and airy, with its veranda and its armchairs, the perfect flower beds are all imprisoned in ten acres. That's what remains from the squandering, the successive re-mortgaging, the divisions and sales of tracts of land. Expenditure was steadily reduced, naturally, but never stopped altogether, just as interest payments never ended, nor fines, nor penalties. With a prestigious family name to bargain with, loans flowed freely from the nouveaux riches, in turn seduced by the opportunity to acquire properties graced with an aura of high society. But as collateral diminished, the lending tap tightened.

Amancio is a classic case, but with his quick temper and aggressive nature, he can only see his situation through a veil of resentment, he regards it all as some dirty trick played by life, putting money in the hands of nobodies while taking it away from those who deserve it by birthright. From his privileged past he retains only the self-confident, back-slapping manner of the affluent Barrio Norte, as well as the haughtiness and effrontery.

When one is born rich, living poor is perceived as an injustice. Everyone should get what they deserve, and Amancio feels he deserves a better life than this. He thinks about tomorrow and tomorrow means Biterman, the moneylender. Amancio has to go to Biterman's office in Once, where the loan shark manages his millions. He has been reduced to borrowing from this Jew, accepting his terms and conditions and the accompanying sense of dependency and inferiority. Only yesterday the bank refused to extend Amancio's overdraft, despite the fact that the president of the bank is none other than Mariano Alzaga, Amancio's cousin and one-time classmate at Saint Andrew's School. Amancio can't even afford a taxi to the *moishe's* office. One more whisky and the bottle is finished. He's completely drunk. Down on the street, the soldiers have stopped a Fiat 1500 and forced two young men to get out.

He looks at Lara's stunning body as she sleeps calmly. She's young, an outstanding beauty even in a family famous for its beautiful women, the jewels at gatherings held in their mansion on Alvear Street. The Cernadas-Bauers had also descended into bankruptcy, but its women were as resourceful as they were lovely to look at, because somewhere on the family tree their proud Galician blood had mixed with pragmatic German genes. Hence the implacable green eyes and blond hair and a dynamic entrepreneurial streak. Lara's sister Florencia used her family connections to set up an estate agency. The sway of her hips, allied with the niceties and histrionics of a well-bred girl, seduced buyers and sellers alike, boosting her client list and her commissions. Without becoming rich, she had made herself into a woman of means for the price of a demanding job on

19

the property market. Lara, on the other hand, with her more fiery, less organized spirit, opted for the shortest route. Following various affairs with men and women of the jet set, in exchange for gifts and favours, she had become a prime topic of conversation among the chattering classes with talk of her prostituting her heritage. So she accepted a position as private secretary to a Harvard-educated executive with a Polish surname, who managed the Argentine outlet of Exxon with great expertise. Lara had no particular aptitude or knowledge for the job, but her salary recognized that her role was to serve the Pole in every kind of way and, with minimum fuss, she carried out certain tasks his wife was disinclined towards. The actors change roles but the plot remains the same. They have both been living off Lara's salary for several months. Amancio has known her since she was a girl, the life and soul of gatherings of mutual acquaintances, social events at his or her parents' ranch. For as long as he could, Amancio passed himself off in front of her as a man of considerable standing, and thus squandered his last remaining pesos in courting and entertaining her. A couple of visits to Europe, various other trips and excursions, expensive clothes and cosmetics, and he was ruined. But before her suitor's bankruptcy became obvious, Lara followed her father's advice and decided to marry into the good family name of Pérez Lastra, finally putting a stop to the gossip doing the rounds of Recoleta, Palermo Chico, the old quarter, and Las Lomas de San Isidro. Marriage gave her the benefit of status along with a good lifestyle, all for the price of putting up with her consort. But she'd been misled. Now that the wealthy disguise has peeled away, revealing the wrinkles and cracks of a bygone era, Lara searches with growing impatience for an honourable means of escape from this inconvenient union. The Pole has more problems with his wife by the day and, as a consequence, more problems with Lara, and she sees the ship on the horizon, starting to sink.

Amancio stealthily makes his way to the dresser where Lara has left her handbag. He opens the clasp carefully. Feeling around in the dark, he soon finds her purse. He takes it out. In the half-light, he makes out three ten-thousand peso notes. He takes one, tucks it in his pocket and puts the purse back in place. He passes the drinks cabinet on his way back and unenthusiastically serves himself a cognac before returning to his post at the window.

The military jeeps and soldiers have gone, the Fiat and its occupants disappeared. The street lies empty and silent. Night draws on, darkens. Those who can, sleep

3

A harsh wind starts to blow. Several broken clouds rush across the sky. Major Giribaldi wanders nervously through the hospital gardens. Tonight's the night, they said. He believes he's found the answer to his wife's problems. He's only forty years old but he's feeling more like seventy. He's impatient. He searches among the many pockets of his uniform for the cigarette he cadged off a conscript. He's not a smoker but in situations like this you smoke. So he smokes. The moon pokes out between the branches of the tall trees lining Luis María Campos and reminds Giribaldi of a similar moon, four years ago.

Ay lunita tucumana, hand in hand with Maisabé on the banks of the river, Giribaldi sings of the Tucumán moon, swears his undying love, whatever it takes to get her into bed. Courting Maisabé involved accompanying her home from church every Sunday and adopting an overall approach that was so roundabout it took him six months before he dared touch a breast for the first time. Even then he knew he risked losing her for ever. She let him get away with it up to a certain point, then stopped him cold, with a firm virginal hand, and he could advance no further. Maisabé's Catholic convictions were stronger than the hot flushes he managed, through great effort, to coax from her. He could always get only so far: her panting, cheeks on fire, nipples stiff as steel and then the *that's enough Giri!* that sounded like a warning of land mines ahead. For a whole year he was unable to get any further. Desire got the better of him, meaning the altar. Sick of masturbating and tired of the *chinitas*, the Indian girls down the local brothel, that night, under that moon, he asked Maisabé to marry him. Emotional and reduced to tears, she accepted immediately. The soldier advanced another pigeon step: with faint hand, Maisabé barely touched his desperate sex, then pulled her hand away like a startled fish. Such was the progress he made from his proposal of marriage.

So then came asking permission of her parents, authorization from his superiors, the white dress, the church, the party and then, finally, the surrender. Alone together as husband and wife, she moved straight to penetration and then as abruptly reached a standstill. It was all very brief. Quick relief for Giribaldi, and for Maisabé one more wifely duty performed before God. Afterwards, the groom, half-asleep, couldn't help asking himself if it had all been worth it. When he awoke, he found Maisabé kneeling at the end of the bed, praying. He took her by the hand with a commanding gesture, brought her back to bed and hugged her tight. She snuggled up to him, looked at him with sad black eyes and said nothing. For Giribaldi, the closeness of this fresh body, unspoilt and so long yearned for, and now so very still and glued to him, began to excite him. And so, as gently as possible, he pushed himself away from her, rolled over and went to sleep.

Their amorous encounters are not as frequent or intense as Giribaldi would like. Maisabé never takes the initiative, never offers the slightest seductive gesture, never even a caress. He always has to get things started then lead all the way. At some point she will pant for a moment, before her regular breathing promptly returns. That's it for her part. Climax is her husband's domain, something she bares in silent, still resignation. She has never been told pleasure forms part of God's plan. And so pleasure is not for her. Afterwards, she waits for her husband to fall asleep before kneeling and praying for forgiveness, her body full of anguish. Giribaldi longs for what he has never had, a satisfied woman, with no strength left for anything, abandoning herself and her thoughts entirely to her man, kisses like in the movies. But it would never be like this with Maisabé. Not with her. Nor with any other woman, there is no other woman, nor even the possibility or the thought. Giribaldi knows not the art of seduction.

About a year ago he resorted to the child argument. This would sanctify their union because it was part of God's plan, and so it served as a foil to increase the frequency, if not the intensity, of their lovemaking. But it also led down another path. Despite their best efforts, Maisabé didn't get pregnant. They calculated the days, asked for advice, went to consultants, all to no avail. Her body was fine: all systems go, according to the fertility analysis. Everything was as it should be, but pregnancy just wouldn't come and with every menstruation Maisabé sank into a deeper pool of despair. Giribaldi agreed, with some reluctance, to a sperm test. He was given the all-clear too. But still nothing. The doctor said the problem must lie elsewhere and so Maisabé started to feel guilty and Giribaldi exploited this guilt by having his way with her more regularly. This satisfied him for a while, Maisabé being a devout and self-sacrificing woman, but the regular monthly frustration, her periods denouncing her infertility, diminished her will and their amorous encounters soon became poisoned with varying degrees of shame and resentment. The military doctor who was helping them, with all the discretion that corresponded to his rank, spoke to Giribaldi of his experience: *many women who can't get pregnant despite being organically capable decide to adopt. Once they have adopted, as if by magic, they end up getting pregnant themselves. I'd bet my life that'd be the case with Maisabé. Adopt, Major, and you'll see how everything falls into place. What's more, adoption is the easiest thing in the world these days.* Giribaldi put the idea to Maisabé, who agreed, with a timid nod of the head. And so he finds himself in the gardens of the Military Hospital. Pregnant fair-haired prisoners are generally sent there to give birth.

Forty days ago, a girl of around twenty was brought in from COTI Martínez, the secret detention centre. Pitocin ran through her veins, forcing the contractions along in ever more frequent waves. The doctor, somewhat distractedly, monitored the dilation process. She dealt with her labour pains with a defeated and distant attitude but she collaborated towards the birth with determination. She was dying to see her child. Yet when the baby started to come out, when her efforts were no longer required, Pentotal did its thing and she fell into a chemical sleep, in what the medical world would describe as "an induced coma".

Earlier today, the doctor came for the child, claiming he had to vaccinate it. The girl watched them take her baby away and knew, knew, knew that was the end, but she tried to expel this thought from her head and later, she let them take her somewhere they said would be more comfortable for her to nurture her child. Off she went, resisting the certainty that she would never see her infant again, that she would never be coming back.

Now the child is in Giribaldi's arms, along with a bag, a few rushed instructions and the address of a trusted paediatrician. Next it will go to the Major's home, where Maisabé is waiting, kneeling and praying.

Giribaldi arrives and places the baby on the coffee table, like an offering. He practically has to drag the frightened Maisabé over to meet it. On seeing the little thing asleep, a bittersweet smile spreads across her face. Then the baby stirs, opens its eyes and wails hard. Maisabé recoils, stumbles and falls, landing on her backside. She covers her eyes with both hands.

It hates me; it knows I am not its real mother.

When Giribaldi takes Maisabé out of the living room, the baby stops crying.

4

There's nothing like a well-timed death. When stars die at the pinnacle of their careers, before the ageing process has reared its ugly head to disappoint the fans, they stay on top for ever, suspended in the popular imagination, adored in life and idolized in death by the masses. Like Gardel dying in the plane crash. Like Marisa. She died at the very moment Lascano loved her most. A traffic accident. Simple, quick, brutal, irreparable. She left and every comfort, every happiness, everything went with her. Everything lost.

At first the shock had stunned him, left him disorientated, detached from reality. Then a blind fury awoke in him, directed at everyone and no one, but mainly against himself. Then her absence became a knife to the chest, twisting deeper by the day. He was unable to resign himself to his fate and began to regret his lack of religion, finding himself wanting to believe in a God he could blame and curse. He fondly contemplated his Bersa, picturing his brains splattered across the bed, so incomplete without Marisa.

This was when Fuseli stepped in. He read the symptoms and saw where they were leading. On the pretext of having nowhere to live, Fuseli asked if he could stay with Lascano for a while, as a favour to a friend. Not having the strength to say no, Lascano fell for the trick, which would save his life. Fuseli took charge of protecting Lascano from himself. With perfect patience, Fuseli brought him from the depths of despair back to the surface where life, absurdly, continued. Lascano recovered because his friend gave him something to believe in, something to hold on to. Fuseli appealed to Lascano's sense of justice and Perro clung on, in desperation, to what became his mission in life: making the world a fairer place, even if only a little. A bit ridiculous perhaps, but as good a lifeline as any. Mission accomplished, Fuseli went home, back to his solitude, leaving Lascano to his.

Marisa had been a star for him only, adored by the masses – of one, Lascano. Destiny never allowed them the time to tire of one another, for daily routine to overshadow the magic moments that bound them. Conjugal life had not yet worn down their love; over-familiarity had not diluted the mystery. Eight years after their wedding, on the edge of the precipice, which claims most marriages, maybe just moments before irremediable boredom set in, she went and died.

His soul refused to accept it and stubbornly raved delirious, imagining a recovered Marisa, a resurrection, a miraculous second chance. Back by his side, to accompany him through the rest of his days until he becomes intolerable, poisoned with old age. Back with him until their love reaches its final thread, a love that was left with no outlet just when it was ready to peak. Back so he can love her so much that it becomes impossible to love her more, or so that he can just love her. So that she can become his constant companion, until having her by his side becomes taken for granted, taken as given. Until her most intimate habits hold no secret, until not a single fold of her skin remains unexplored. So that he can say to her all the words that now choke him. Until her sex loses any taste of the new, any sense of discovery. Until he no longer notices her smell and her voice becomes as familiar as his own. Until he knows what she's going to say before she says it. Until understanding comes without even needing to look at each other. Until she becomes as familiar to him as the atmosphere itself, he stops sensing her presence and she becomes but an appendix to him. Until he guiltily lusts after, even has, other women. Until they become strangers eating in passive silence in restaurants, having given up wondering what they are doing there one with the other. Until it is she who's left standing alone at the end of the pier when his ship sails.

But there'd be none of this. Their future suspended, finished, buried under a small gravestone in the Jewish cemetery that he never visits, because he knows she's not really there. Instead, she visits him during his interminable nights, sometimes as a painful presence, sometimes as a lascivious phantom that possesses him. His body remembers her body as if it's been tattooed onto him, making her presence real, lifting his sex and squeezing his hand until his hand is her hand. In the darkness, in the silence, while the furniture in the flat creaks, she makes love to him and leaves him feeling more alone than ever. He curses her a thousand times because her absence forces him to confront true solitude every night, and he wishes he had never met her. To go on as he was before Marisa, when solitude was his natural state, his habitat, an environment he lived in without even fully sensing it. After her... after her, Lascano falls asleep.

Crack. He wakes up. The sound of footsteps on pine floorboards reverberates in his ears like a gunshot. The flat lies silent. Someone is walking around. He gets out of bed. Hiding behind the door, he sees a shadow in the lounge. He leans against the wall. His eyes mist over. It's Marisa. She appears to be rearranging things, but the things don't move. She has her back to him, with her nightgown on, the thick winter one, although it doesn't hide the curves of her body. Lascano feels as though a stake has been plunged into his chest. Marisa turns around. There's a distance in her eyes, a sadness, a pain, an absence... He sits down and looks at her. He knows if he speaks to her she won't answer. She's barefoot, as she always is. She stands still a moment, then starts to sway, dancing without moving her feet, rocking her empty arms. Perro thinks he can hear a sad song playing. He covers his eyes with his hands, but he still sees her. She encourages a reluctant little boy to come out from behind her skirt and show himself. He has his mother's eyes. Marisa acts like nothing has changed, like she's still alive. She does it for Lascano, so that he doesn't feel so alone, so awful, so sad, but these visits pain him. He'd rather not see her. *Leave me be*, he thinks, recalling the popular bolero: *Vete de mí.* And she does leave him be, disappearing into the kitchen, and then when he looks in there she's gone again, and he hears her singing in the bathroom, *Tú, que llenas todo de alegría y juventud: you fill everything with happiness and youth.* When he goes into the bathroom she's not there. He hears her in the room. He follows her sounds but she's not there. He collapses on his bed in need of respite. Then she enters, slips under the sheets and Lascano's body does the rest, without being able to help it, surrendering himself to the ghost, knowing he'll pay dearly for it .

Showing all the signs of a sleepless night and a full day at work, Lascano heads over to Fuseli's house, a small one-bedroom apartment with a huge terrace, on the corner of Agüero and Córdoba. Fuseli leans on the balcony railing and calmly waits for his friend to say whatever it is he's come to say. Lascano, meanwhile, whimsically looks over at the Ameghino Mental Health Centre across the street, with its tumbledown gardens and peeling walls, and imagines himself a boarder there. The night is clear, fresh and still.

Fuseli, do you believe in ghosts?

The doctor takes his time to answer, eventually raising his eyes and pointing upwards.

What do you see? The sky. And in the sky? Stars. You think you see stars, but you're mistaken. Stop fucking about, she visited me again last night. Marisa? Who else? OK, but you asked me if I believed in ghosts. And you started banging on about the stars. Bear with me: many of those stars you think you see actually disappeared millions of years ago. How can they have disappeared if I'm looking at them right now? Because what you see is the light of those stars. I don't get you. It's very simple. Well go on then. A star emits light, right? Right. Light travels through space, right? Right. The star dies, right? OK. The light reaches you. Yes. But the star died long ago. Shit. That light is the ghost of the dead star.

Lascano sparks up a cigarette, his gaze lost somewhere among the pattern of the floor tiles. Fuseli, seeing the reaction of his friend, inflates like a frog and adopts his most solemn and doctorly tone.

Every life form, simply by being alive, emits energy that projects itself into space. Like with the stars, this energy keeps on travelling, maybe does so eternally, even once the thing that emitted it has long gone. Marisa died, we both know that, but her energy keeps reaching you. And Marisa was a very bright being. All the time you were together, your body was training itself to receive her signals, so now you're like an antenna for her energy waves that carry on flying around your house. When everything else in the flat is turned off, and you relax and let your guard down, that's when her signals reach you, like the light of a dead star. That's what ghosts are.

Lascano takes a deep puff of his cigarette. Fuseli looks like a professor giving a seminar.

But she does things, she gets into my bed. That, my friend, is your crazy little head. When you receive her signals, memories come back to you, fantasies, your body's recollections of the feelings she used to stir in you, the emotions. The mind loves to make up stories and it starts spinning a yarn, giving shape to an explanation for what you're sensing. When someone leaves us, they leave us with a void we didn't have when they were there. Our emotions end up with no place to go because we no longer have someone to direct them towards. You're on your own... Our other half is our great witness, the keeper of our imagination, the one who confirms that our world is real, concrete, palpable. Our other half is the key piece of our universe. You ask: Did you see that? Did you hear that? What do you think about that? Our other half provides us with the only proof we ever get that what we sense is real.

The friends remain silent. The wind starts to blow, night deepens. Fuseli seems woken from a dream.

You're still suffering from Marisa's death. Pain has the virtue of making people deeper beings. Suffering makes the good guys more compassionate, more noble; it makes the bad guys worse, more perverse, more wicked. So what can I do about it? Just stay calm. Trying to resist will only make it worse. In time it will pass. Right now I've got a lovely bottle of red waiting to be drunk and a pork loin stuffed with pineapple cooking in the oven, which it would be plain stupid to eat on my own. You fancy tackling it with me? Did you wash your hands after work? Are you crazy? That's where the extra flavour comes from.

5

A sticky night descends on the city. Eva is out on the terrace gathering in the washing when she hears engines and people running in the street. She peeks out cautiously. The house is being surrounded by soldiers dressed in army fatigues and carrying rifles. The olive-green bonnet of an army truck pokes around the corner. Twenty soldiers fan out in formation. An armoured car crosses the road, demolishes the railings, ploughs across the garden, charges the door and sends it flying, then pulls back quickly. The troops advance shooting. Physical fear takes control of her muscles, emptying her mind of any thought other than the need to flee. She leaps down the staircase that gives on to the backyard, gets a foot up on the gas pipes and climbs the dividing wall, jumping down into the neighbouring garden. She sprints across it and scales another dividing wall. An Alsatian jumps up at her from the shadows and she avoids its jaws by a whisker. A light comes on and a voice calls out, which distracts the dog for a split second, allowing Eva to duck into a passageway and shut the gate behind her. Away from the angry barking, she scampers up a staircase and onto a rooftop, where she waits to get her breath back.

Glued to the wall, she feels like an animal pursued by a pack of hounds, fleeing from the gunshots that ring out into the night sky and echo off the river. She comes across an empty room and enters. There are long make-up tables with mirrors and lights, like a theatre dressing room. She drops into a chair. She doesn't even recognize her reflection in the mirror, her face is so distorted by fear. She holds her head in her hands and starts to cry. Outside, the gun battle draws to an end with the final, sporadic *coups de grâce*. Far off, she hears the sound of the movement of troops, motors, muffled orders. Completely exhausted and her mind a blank, her body shuts down and she dozes.

Two days ago, Manuel, her partner, her friend, her companion, ran into an army ambush. She thinks of him and Silvio, lying in a street in Tigre like discarded objects, in puddles of blood. Manuel's death pains her in the head but not in the heart, because her love for him died the last time they saw each other, the last time they would ever have each other, when she told him and he wouldn't listen. Because Manuel barely ever listened to her, obsessed as he was with a cruel determination to change the world, whatever it took.

Something alerts her. Voices from the stairwell, approaching. She stands up. She looks for a place to hide, the voices getting ever closer. Like a mouse, she scurries under the make-up table and pulls a chair in front of her. From her hiding place she sees the legs of two women who come through the door talking loudly.

You see the shit that went down over there? I heard the shots. Seems like the military busted a hide-out. Crooks? Guerrillas. What happened? How the hell should I know? I was hardly going to go over and ask.

38

Another woman comes in and sits down on the seat in front of Eva, who has to press herself right up against the wall to avoid the woman's legs. They change out of their simple street clothes, putting on provocative sequined dresses and make-up. A very young-sounding girl bursts in.

What's with the long faces, girls? Didn't you hear? Hear what? She lives on a different planet. Darling, they just busted some subversives over there and shot everyone to shit. Don't tell me we're not going to be able to work tonight? I've got to pay the kid's school tomorrow or they're kicking him out. Don't ask me. We'll have to wait and see what Tony says.

Eva turns towards the sound of approaching footsteps. A man enters, dressed in red trousers, socks and shoes.

Says about what? Are we going to be able to work tonight? And why the hell not? No, just that we were wondering, because of the shooting. Don't worry about that. The Major in charge is a friend of mine. Who do you think tipped them off in the first place? Tony's always on top of things. All right, enough with the chat and get to work, it's going to be a long night. We're going, we're going.

The man hurries them out of the room, then shouts something Eva can't make out. He comes back immediately with another man.

Shut the door. How did it go? No problem. You got the dough? Here you are. Did you count it? Did you ask me to count it? Yes. Then I counted it. Twenty grand. Was the old guy happy? When he saw the two little black girls, he was practically drooling. Did he say anything? No, he just gave me the cash and chucked me out. Good, well go downstairs and keep an eye on things. I'm on my way. Did you speak to the army boys? The coast's clear. Good. Shut the door behind you.

Tony goes over to the wall in front of Eva and crouches down. Her heart stops as she thinks she's been discovered, but the man is struggling with a socket, which he pulls away to reveal a safe deposit box. He opens the box and puts two wads of cash inside, fixes the socket back in place, gets up and leaves. Eva is on the point of choking, she can't tell how long she's been holding her breath.

Lascano strolls across Vicente López square, where rich families' dogs are brought to shit by maids in aprons. The maids earn a tenth of what gets spent on these fine specimens, the more exotic the better. Smoking a cigarette in the shade of a giant rubber tree, Lascano is pleased to see that his men are at the ready. He has been tailing Tony Ventura for eight months. Now he has him. He walks calmly and smokes a cigarette while his men take up their final positions on the corner of Gaspar Campos and Arredondo. Ventura runs his business right here in a plush mansion he's managed to get hold of through some shady dealing. Mortgaged to the hilt, it's perfect for the high-class brothel he's set up, at least until they get evicted. Tony's convinced that having powerful people as clients covers him against police raids and judicial intervention. Carried away with his sense of impunity, he expanded operations into the traffic of cocaine, high-stakes poker tables and, for his sins, underage prostitution. The last development finally convinced the judge to sign the search warrant.

The previous summer, at Punta del Este, Justice Marraco watched as Mariana, his thirteen-year-old daughter, blossomed. At La Brava beach, she wore a bikini, which struggled to contain her adolescent tits. Her little bum filled out and an incipient fuzz of straight hairs began to poke out of the sides of her tiny panties. He had never seen a woman with straight hair down there before. Her mouth became ripe, her eyes suggestive and one morning he found her knickers stained with blood. She was a young woman now. It started to send Marraco crazy when he caught men staring at her; even his best friends ogled his little girl's body. Jealousy stuck its teeth in and wouldn't let go. He tried to force his daughter to wear a more discreet bathing suit, but all this achieved was to send her, with increasing regularity, to another beach, another stage on which to play out this drama, far away from prying paternal eyes. One night, arriving home from the San Rafael casino, Marraco looked through the window and saw one of the Pertinetti boys groping her on the living room couch. She, happy as can be; her mother, complicit; Marraco, furious.

Ventura picked up three fifteen-year-old girls in Asunción, bought for the price of two. Of Guarani Indian and German stock, these dark-skinned girls, with their smooth, jet-black hair and green eyes, could easily pass for Thai. In some form or other, Tony was continuing a tradition established in the Twenties and Thirties by *Zwi Migdal*, the Jewish mafia, who smuggled in blond Poles who could pose as French maids in Buenos Aires.

Lascano has a search warrant in his pocket, signed by Marraco and his paranoia. Even if such documents had fallen into disuse, it protected Perro should he end up in front of some government heavyweight or a member of the armed forces.

The uniformed policemen grow impatient, lying in wait a few yards from the house where Eva hides. Lascano waves to them and some salute him, but he's not really paying attention. He heads over to the deputy superintendent.

Everyone in position? We're all ready, Superintendent. Just give the order. Let's wait for the judge to get here.

The officer's expression is a mixture of amazement and resignation at the words of his superior: he's not used to a judge being present on a raid. For him, judges are the men who usually just show up in the newspapers taking the credit for everything once the dirty work's been done. He feels no particular inclination to ask questions. He prefers the quiet life and so he limits himself to responding with courtesy and subordination:

Whatever you say, sir.

In the back seat of a Falcon, driven by a policeman Lascano has seen once or twice before, Marraco arrives with Arrechea, one of his clerks. As Lascano heads over to the car, the judge lowers the window.

Good evening, Judge. How are you, Lascano? How's everything going? We're all ready. Ventura's inside and there are signs of life in the house. Do you think they'll put up a fight? These people are not especially violent, but you never know. In any case, we're well prepared. Are you going to join in with the operation? I would love to see Ventura's face when we cuff him. That'll teach him what you get when you mess with minors. But I can't. Mr Arrechea here will accompany you. As you wish. Anyway, tomorrow you'll give me all the details. Of course, your honour.

Marraco puts his window up and signals to the chauffeur to get going. He wants to be home fast, to monitor his daughter's activities. The car pulls away and melts into the shadows, periodically reappearing in the glow of the traffic lights at every junction, shrinking each time until it disappears. Arrechea doesn't like the way he is being treated like a child.

Right sir, here's how it's going to work. We'll go in and secure the place. When we're sure the situation is under control, I'll send someone out to get you and we can start proceedings. I

don't want to put you at any risk. Does that seem OK to you?
It seems fine. Then let's get moving. Attack positions everyone.
At the ready.

With a gesture of the hand, Perro orders two men with a battering ram to smash down the door.

Eva leaves her hiding place to peek down the stairwell and hears voices of men and women down below. There's a sudden explosion, the crash of the door as it's bashed in. Running and yelling.

The party's over. Lascano blocks the exit, cigarette hanging out of his mouth, and enjoys watching his operation unfold, designed to perfection. In a matter of minutes, whores and clients are identified and Ventura is handcuffed and brought out to Perro, who can't help but smile: dressed all in red, Ventura looks like a toy devil. Lascano covers his mouth, coughs and orders his men to let those they've arrested put their clothes back on. An officer whispers something in the superintendent's ear.

Let them go.

Lascano pretends not to notice as two men, heads bowed, hurry out the door and disappear into the street.

Night's drawn in on you, Ventura. The game's up.

Although a tall man, Ventura seems to have shrunk in defeat.

Nice outfit, Tony. Do they do one for men? Fuck you, Perro...
Superintendent Lascano to you... There must be some way we can settle this. The only person who's going to settle this is Judge Marraco, and you should see how mad he gets when minors are involved. Take him away.

On the top floor, Eva hears footsteps coming up the stairs. She quietly shuts the door. She goes back to her hiding place under the table. She pulls the chair back in front of her. She sits on the floor and waits with her hands clasped together, as if praying, although she doesn't pray. A policeman enters, walks around the room, then leaves and Eva sighs in relief.

Down below, the policemen herd whores, pimps and clients away. The officer, back from upstairs, heads over to Lascano.

All secure, Superintendent. There's no one left up there. Good, take everyone down to headquarters for me.

Arrechea, who has been as still and silent as if at mass, adopts a sudden authoritative pose when Lascano approaches.

Well sir, it's been a complete success. True enough, Lascano, a very tidy operation. Let me suggest you go home to your family now. I'll take charge of the rest of this and send the report to the court in the morning. That's fine. Until tomorrow then. Until tomorrow. Thanks for everything. Not at all.

Lascano smiles to himself. Having quickly rid himself of the clerk, he can now give free rein to his talents as a detective. He examines the house room by room. It's luxurious: the furniture, the pictures on the walls, the upholstery; everything speaks of a wealth accumulated over generations, of studies in Europe, of good breeding. He climbs the grandiloquent marble staircase. He walks around slowly, taking everything in. Eva, still sitting on the floor, hidden under the table, sees his legs come into view and hopes she won't be discovered. He's just a few inches above her head, looking over the objects on the dressing table. He moves away, tapping a small black notebook against his leg. It drops to the floor. As he bends down to pick it up, her whole body involuntarily spasms and her foot moves the seat. Lascano's hand is on his holster in a flash. He approaches and kicks the chair away, revealing a young woman with her face turned to the floor. Eva looks up and meets the policeman's eyes. Perro's heart stops. It's Marisa, his dead wife. The face, the hair, the shoulders, the hands, the complexion. That slightly defiant, slightly melancholic air, but above all else, the eyes: it's Marisa.

The spell is suddenly broken by the voice of Sergeant Molinari, who, from where he stands, can't see what has stunned Lascano. He has come to inform his superintendent that the prisoners have all been taken away. Lascano, without taking his eyes off the girl, tells them to get going, *I'll catch you up*. Alone once more in silence, he looks at the woman in amazement.

Here, hidden under the table of a high class brothel, is Marisa, staring right back at him. Lascano realizes he's lost control of the situation, doesn't know what to do. He reaches out and touches her hair, just to be sure she's real. He can't arrest her, he can't set her free, he can't pretend not to have seen her. When she tries to speak, he raises a finger to his lips. He takes her by the hand and helps her up, wraps her in his overcoat and leads her out of the house, without saying a word. Outside rages the stupidity of men, running around, killing each other over money.

The girl puts up no protest. She occasionally aims a furtive glance at Lascano, trying to guess his intentions. Scared, she considers trying to escape, but decides the odds are against her. It's impossible to decipher this man, who's old enough to be her father, smokes incessantly and treats her like a lady in waiting. When they pull on to Libertador, she fears he's taking her to be interrogated at the torture chambers of E.S.M.A, the

Navy Mechanics School, but they drive straight past. Then she thinks they must be going to the dreaded military intelligence unit at Batallón 601 headquarters at the intersection of Viamonte and Callao, but they pull on to Avenida Juan B. Justo. He eventually parks up in La Paternal. In this neighbourhood there is no secret military prison she knows of, *but who knows how many there are?* Once out on the street, he walks five paces in front of her, she thinks of running, *but where to?* She stops. He walks straight ahead, not once turning round. Frightened, intrigued and trembling with cold, she follows Perro all the way into his apartment.

Have a hot shower. It'll do you some good. Here's a towel and a dressing gown.

Lascano looks at the bird in the cage. The animal jumps around nervously, then lets out a *tweet* of recognition. Lascano shakes his head and goes into the kitchen. He feels dizzy. He puts a pot of water on the stove. He lights the gas and a cigarette with the same match, allows his mind to rest, lulled by the hiss of the flame. As the water comes to the boil, he turns off the gas, the flame burning out in a tiny explosion. He prepares the *mate*, a methodical ritual.

He's sitting on the sofa when she returns from her shower. She looks even more like Marisa than she did before, more everyday. He passes her the *mate*.

What's your name? Eva. Are you hungry?

She nods her head. Perro gets up from his seat. From the sofa, Eva can see him preparing some food. She can't understand what's going on. After a while, Lascano comes back with two steaming plates of spaghetti in a tomato sauce and places them one across from the other on the wobbly coffee table. He goes back into the kitchen, comes out with a bottle of wine, two glasses and cutlery, and leaves them all in a muddle on the table. He sits down, starts eating and signals for Eva to do the same. She dives in. The basic, simple food tastes delicious. Eva lingers over the flavours, feeling the nourishment bringing her strength back, and her body yearns for more. A sip of wine immediately puts colour in her cheeks. A sense of warmth and well-being awakens in her, until now but a distant memory, hidden between the folds of a desolate present. She wonders, *How have I ended up here?* Lascano makes the most of her being so distracted to stare at her. He feels like he's reliving the first time he cooked for Marisa. The only thing missing is for her to say:

Mmm, the pasta's perfect, al dente.

And for him to answer:

Well, I am a hard-boiled detective.

Normally, witty replies came to him hours or even days after the event, but not on that occasion, laughter springing forth as if a magic spell had been cast upon both of them. Lascano smiles sadly to himself, a gesture that doesn't escape Eva's attention, although she doesn't understand it, nor feel the need to. There's something happening here. She doesn't know what it is, but she likes it, finds it comforting, it makes her feel at home. She doesn't know why, but this man fills her with a sense of security. Very suddenly, Lascano gets to his feet and goes into the bedroom, then comes back again with a blanket which he throws next to her on the sofa.

So that you don't get cold... Sleep for now and we'll decide what to do with you in the morning.

He goes back into his room and closes the door. Eva remains still for a few moments. She hears some movement in the bedroom. Then silence. Empty plates. She stands up. She picks up the dishes, goes into the kitchen, washes them; she has to do something. In the distance, machine guns rattle.

In his bed, Lascano begins to doze. Marisa smiles at him. He turns over. He slips his hand under his body, slowly, until it reaches his sleeping sex. He wakes it up, knowing, like a humming bird flying backwards, where to find Marisa, open and defenceless and selfless and needy and warm and hospitable and familiar, and inhabits her body as if it were a house, and he lets desire take control of him and his heart sinks and he cries, and in the distance machine guns rattle.

6

In Once, the Jewish quarter of Buenos Aires, after the shops have pulled down their shutters, the pavements overflow with left-over fabrics, rolls of cardboard and other unwanted material thrown out by the shop-keepers. Men, women and children dig through the waste, fishing out anything useful or anything that can be sold to the recycling plant for a few coins per kilo Such enterprising families manage to survive by sifting through other people's rubbish. Thus the police in the Seventh district receive their bribes not as protection money but for turning a blind eye to this practice.

Rich Jewish families have begun a slow but irreversible exodus: they keep their businesses in Once but prefer to live in Barrio Norte or Belgrano, districts of greater social prestige. The elderly are left behind, in once luxurious buildings of the Golden Age, the founders of the fortunes that now pay for huge flats overlooking Libertador Avenue, holidays in Punta del Este, imported cars and private education at supposed British schools. The younger generation never loses sleep worrying about how to scrimp and save; indeed they revel in flaunting their wealth. Children of affluence, who never experienced the privations of the war, the miseries of the *pogroms*, the phantasmagoria of the concentration camps, they are busy acting grand. They think good living means spending more. There are quite a few exceptions. Elías Biterman is one of them.

This is one of those moments of dead time in Biterman's life. He tries to avoid these empty hours. They are the flanks used by the occupying forces of his memory to attack the haven that is his life in the present. His mind wanders back to when he was very young, crowded together with hundreds of fellow Jews in a caged train, watched over by SS soldiers with machine guns. The train crossed the countryside without stopping at stations, Polish Catholics greeting the passing convoy with chants about Zyklon B and crematorium ovens. They were headed for a concentration camp near Oswiecim, christened Auschwitz by the Nazis. When he read the sign above the gate, *Arbeit macht frei,* and saw the state of the prisoners, he knew he would have to escape as soon as possible, while he still had the strength and the will to try.

His father, Shlomo, a survivor of the Ukrainian *pogroms,* had been alert to what was going on in Germany in the Forties. By lining the pockets of an official at the embassy, he managed to obtain Argentine passports for him and his wife.

Years earlier, during the depression, Shlomo had rescued Heinz Schultz from poverty. Shlomo gave him food, work and board without asking for much in return, until Schultz was tempted by the most patriotic of callings: a position as a guard at Auschwitz. Before leaving a Germany adorned with the ubiquitous swastika, Shlomo got in touch with Heinz and gave him a bundle of *Reichsmarks* and the promise of more if he facilitated Elías's escape.

Schultz shared the money with his colleagues and one night Elías was pulled out of the stalag barrack where he was kept. The rest of the prisoners, accustomed to people being taken away and never coming back, lamented his ill luck and shamefully rejoiced in their own relief. Elías was hidden in the false floor of a provisions truck and taken to a nearby wood. There, the driver took his photo alongside a smiling Schultz. When Elías saw his captors' hands move towards their holsters, he didn't hesitate. He punched Schultz on the nose with all his might and set off running into the forest, into the night, weaving between the trees as they lit up with the flash of gunshot. Not all the bullets missed: one passed through his shoulder and entered his lung. But he was young then, strong and determined. He carried on running and running until he collapsed in a clearing.

Using the photo to get the rest of the reward money, Schultz assured Shlomo that Elías was hiding in a safe place waiting to leave the country. Biterman senior doubled the prize on condition that Schultz passed on a weighty sum to Elías so that he could buy a passport from Vignes, the Consul at the Argentine embassy.

Hopeful he'd done enough for his son and not daring to stay any longer for fear of being denounced, Shlomo and his wife began their arduous pilgrimage to Buenos Aires. Three years later, tired of the persecutions and penuries, he died, leaving his wife four months pregnant.

Naturally, Schultz kept all the extra money and, furthermore, used what he'd been told to extort the embassy official. With his small fortune, Schultz opened a factory making saucepans and kitchen utensils. His contacts provided slave labour from the concentration camps and soon his factory was supplying the front line. Sick of the sweet smell of burnt flesh that billowed from the chimneys of the crematorium, he bought a medical certificate and was discharged from active service. He became rich, but the stench remained stuck up his nose, until the 28 May 1969, when he put the barrel of his Walther PPK between his teeth and pulled the trigger. His children inherited the business and became, with the passing of time, prosperous industrialists, extremely concerned with the quality of their products, which they exported all over the world.

Elías, on the other hand, was rescued by a group of bandits with a den in the heart of the forest. They were natural enemies of the established order, no matter the order. They instinctively took the fugitive to be one of their own. His rescue and recovery were not simply a matter of loyalty to some unwritten code, but also they reasoned that a burly, determined lad like Elías would prove a useful addition to the gang. Politics didn't interest them in the slightest, they simply felt an animal aversion to uniforms, whatever the colour. This band of highwaymen usually ambushed isolated Nazi patrols, plundering them for arms and supplies. Their attacks were quick and clinical, sparing no enemy lives nor resulting in casualties of their own. On one of their raids they were surprised by an SS squadron, which had been on their trail. They were decimated. Elías was one of the few survivors. Fleeing through the night, he came upon a village in the early hours and found what would prove to be his safe conduct: a wheelbarrow. With this perfect disguise, he set off along the country pathways. He walked armed with a Luger, stolen from one of the SS. If he sensed that all was lost, he would use it on himself. He decided under no circumstances would he go back to the concentration camp. Whenever he came across soldiers or patrols, he was taken for a villager going about his daily business and treated with casual indifference. When it proved necessary, he stood to attention, raised his right hand and offered the usual *Heil Hitler!* Always pushing his barrow, he headed south. He crossed Czechoslovakia, Hungary and Austria. In Trieste, he abandoned his prop and slipped aboard a boat as a stowaway. He was discovered in Dakar and thrown onto the quay without further ado.

In total, it took him five years to reach Buenos Aires, find his mother, learn of his father's fate and that he had a brother, Horacio. The long years of solitude, living in a state of constant danger, turned Elías into a shy and silent being, one concerned solely with never becoming destitute again. His past is an interminable collection of horrors that deserve only to be cast into oblivion; the future is uncertain and needs securing; the present is a battleground on which to establish your terms of retirement. Thrifty to the point of ridiculousness, everything seems expensive to Elías. When he has to buy a new pair of shoes, he calculates the value of each shoe separately and always, through sheer persistence, obtains substantial discounts on every transaction he makes, though he won't give an inch when people try to negotiate with him. He managed to multiply a hundred times the modest sum of money his mother gave him, thus providing her, his brother and himself with a decent subsistence, one in which they lacked for nothing but in which nothing was ever left over. Until the day of Sara's death, the only time in his life that Elías ever cried, she was very proud of her eldest, recognizing in him the integrity, vision and discipline of her late husband. Women were otherwise an empty chapter in Biterman's life story. Having had no contact with any, he had never acquired the necessary skills for seduction or courtship. As a young man, he appeased his sexual cravings with occasional and hurried visits to cheap prostitutes. His erotic spark soon burned out, a fact that pleased him as it allowed him to spend all his time on what he considered truly important. The opportunity to cut another cost was always a source of great happiness for him.

Elías hears his brother arrive. His face at the door brings him back to the present. Horacio is Elías's exact opposite. When out and about, going from one place to the next, Horacio's route is determined by any attractive woman who crosses his path. He'll follow her for blocks on end chatting her up, until she agrees to go for a coffee or he gives in, tempted by another. With a particular kind of logic, he tries to pick up every woman he meets, a matter of stacking the odds in his favour: *if I throw myself at twenty, thirty or forty women a day, by the law of averages, one or two will succumb to my advances.* Thus his daily routine is dedicated to chasing skirt, and his life is full of women problems. From his mother he inherited his blaze of orange hair. He has an easy smile, dreamy eyes and a dignified demeanour, and he has cultivated a taste for the sort of fine, well-cut clothing that he wears with elegance. But Horacio is a dandy without a penny to his name. His income is like the slow drip of a tap, his expenditure a fireman's hose. Although he doesn't dare try to cheat Elías, he has no scruples when it comes to stealing. He swindles all his female conquests with stories of the need to buy furniture for when they're married, or whatever ruse will make them give him a few pesos.

His preferred hunting ground is the grandstand at the Palermo racecourse, where he gets to rub shoulders with members of the Jockey Club while awaiting the miracle of the forty-to-one horse, which always seems to pull up in the final stretch. There he can admire the blond, beautiful and distant women of Buenos Aires high society, in whom he can only ever inspire a fleeting interest. It was at the racecourse that he met Amancio Pérez Lastra, a jet-set version of himself. With so much in common, they couldn't help but become immediate friends. Horacio would desperately like to bridge the social divide which, deep down, he knows separates them. So, although it irritates him, he's tolerant of Amancio's habitual remark: *you're my only Jewish friend.*

In a further attempt to ingratiate himself, Horacio thought to introduce Amancio to Elías, so providing his friend with a lending source for the funds he needs with such increasing urgency. Horacio also speculates that his brother might pay a commission for his bringing in a new client. He feels he deserves a lot more out of life, and a lot more out of Elías than the meagre salary he receives in exchange for his position as the errand boy that Elías doesn't need. This role was conceded on the insistence of their mother, the only person in the world ever capable of making her eldest spend a penny on something superfluous.

…So? So nothing. What do you mean nothing? Exactly that, nothing, nil, zero. You're not going to give me anything for the client I'm bringing you? Firstly, I already pay you for doing practically nothing, and secondly, the client hasn't even shown up yet, and you already want a commission. Are you trying to say that I'm of no use to you? I get about as much use out of you as you do out of the money I pay you. Which is not enough. It's

hardly my fault that it's not enough. Nothing is ever enough for you. You've too many vices. Yeah, well that's my problem. I couldn't agree more. And if I decided to leave, where else would you find someone you could trust? Look, when I shave in the morning, I'm on my guard, because I don't even trust my own shadow. I've a firm hand on the tiller, and I won't ever let go. And in this world, the tiller means one thing: guelt. *But Elías... Take your sob story to the temple. So you're not going to give me anything at all for this? First let's take a look at the fish, then we'll decide how to cook it. The guy has some land you can take as guarantee on anything you lend him. Leave that side of things to me, I know a bit more about it than you. Fine, but don't forget afterwards. I never forget anything. I particularly never forget how much you already owe me.*

Out on the landing, Amancio stands in front of the door in his best suit, his burglar outfit as he calls it, with a big smile, ringing Biterman's bell, not noticing he's being spied on by the neighbour through the peephole.

That must be your mate. Go and attend to him. Hold on, let's leave him to stew a moment. Did you go and see his land? It's nice, although really the only thing left is the ranch house. Must be ten or twelve acres. It's a bit abandoned but with a little cash you could do it up. Mother would have loved it. Everything involves a little cash with you. What's it called? La Rencorosa: In Spite. What a name. I like it. Let him in and tell him to wait. I'm off to deal with an important internal call.

Biterman grabs the newspaper off the table and, unfastening his trousers, goes and settles himself on the toilet. He has serious constipation problems, so this is a sacred moment. Horacio leaves the room, shutting the office door behind him, then goes to the front door and opens it. Amancio surveys the apartment. It's one of those dark, poky little places with paper-thin walls, everything made to the bare minimum. You couldn't swing a cat in there. The furniture, the few decorations, the curtains, everything looks cheap and worn out, but the place smells of money.

Amancio. Come on in. How's it going man? Surviving. Your brother? He's on a call right now, then he'll see you. The other person rang so it could take a while. Did you go to see the ranch? Yes. And what did you think? The house is good but a bit rundown. With twenty bucks worth of painting and twenty on repairs it would be as good as new. That may well be, but you try getting twenty bucks out of my brother. The man's careful with his money. Any coin that falls into his hands never sees the light of day again. Why is it called La Rencorosa? It's a family story. My mother inherited the land from a spinster aunt but mum didn't like it, never went. The old man took charge and ended up having an affair with some girl out there. She was some chinita *from the village but with a breathtaking body. A bit of a womanizer, was he? And my granddad, and my great granddad, and my brother and me. It's in the blood. Anyway, the story is he got her pregnant so he moved her into the ranch house, which was then called El Vergel: The Orchard. So one dark day gossip got back to my mum. She grabbed a shotgun, jumped in the car and headed for the country. She confronted the* chinita *and, in a fit of pique, gave her such a kicking that the miscarriage spat out. Then she threw her out onto the street. And what did your old man do? Nothing. Never even mentioned it. The only thing he ever said on the subject, until the day he died, was when my mum changed the name and he asked her why she'd called it La Rencorosa. She said: so that you know the next time you do this to me, you'll be the one getting a kicking. Dad kept his gob shut and that was the end of that... Hey, is your brother going to take much longer? I shouldn't think so. Hot-tempered family you've got. We don't*

57

beat about the bush. Did I tell you about the time a farmhand insulted me and I gave him a good whipping?

Elías appears smiling. It went well.

So you must be the famous Amancio. Pleased to meet you. How's everything going? Battling on as usual. Come on through. So how can I be of assistance? Well, I've run into a few financial difficulties. And do these difficulties have a name? Some ten million of them. That's more than a few difficulties. Well, the valuation of La Rencorosa says that I can guarantee that figure, the land is worth ten times more. If you say so. How will you pay me back? I can write cheques. Let's see. OK, write me four cheques for three and a half million each. You're charging me some crazy kind of interest. What's crazy is lending without a guarantee. But I'm guaranteeing them against a splendid country ranch. And how do I know that it's not compromised by several other debts, that tomorrow you won't go bankrupt and I have to get to the back of the creditor queue? But please, you have my word. I can't deposit your word in a bank though can I? This is how it is. Take it or leave it. OK, fine. When can I have the money? Slow down, first you leave me your details and I gather a bit of background information, then you drop in on Berún, the town clerk, Horacio will give you the address, and you sign a property injunction. But I suggest you think this through carefully first, because I have to tell you, I'm not a tolerant man when it comes to missed payments. If you don't pay up, I'll claim for the ranch. I don't care whether you're a friend of my brother's or not, patience is not my best virtue. Mine neither. So how shall we leave it? Once you've been through the formalities with the clerk, come back here to collect the loan. Expenses run on your account. But you leave me the cheques now. And who's to say you don't just keep the cheques and never give me the money? Nobody. And so? Those are the conditions, take them or leave them. Who do I make the cheques out to? The bearer.

7

The pale hours before dawn. Execution hour. For several nights, Giribaldi has neglected his duties as task force commander. He has been granted a few days leave on account of the baby. The Major is asleep in bed with his arms folded, fists clenched. He doesn't hear the siren that crosses the city. The brightness of a new day starts to poke its way through the cracks in the blind. From the street come the sounds of motors, barked orders, rushed steps, troop movements. Maisabé lies awake at her husband's side. Her gaze is fixed on the ceiling, her eyes sore through lack of blinking. She hasn't slept all night.

Oh dear God, I asked you and asked you for a child and now you have sent me one who hates me. It's too young to hate, but I know, it hates me. It must have hatred in the blood. And no, it's not just me imagining things. A mother knows. I know and I don't know what to do. When Giri brought it in, I could see how it looked at me. Yes, it looked at me, eyes wide open. And I'd have liked to have told it not to worry, that I was going to love it as a mother, more than its mother, who couldn't even look after herself, never mind what she'd carried inside her. Our father, who art in heaven. I want to love it. But I just can't. I can't. Hallowed be thy name. So small and yet so big and so knowing, so comprehending. And Giri doesn't understand, because he's a man of action and doesn't think, but I do think. He says I think too much. Thy kingdom come. And when it gets old, if when it gets old it seeks vengeance. If he, for it is also a he, grows up to be a man of action like his father, and all this hate comes pouring out. What then? Thy will be done. What is thy will? That one pays for ever? On earth as it is in heaven. Meaning? If we have done wrong, we pay for it on earth and in heaven. In which case we have to give the baby back. But to who? How? Where do we look? Give us this day our daily bread. The sinning won't end until we return what we've stolen. We've stolen it and now there's no one to give it back to. Give us this day. Yes this day, today, today, while he sleeps in his cot. While I walk to his room. But Lord, if his mother is dead then the only way to give him back is to send him to her. But where is she? Oh the doubts, always the doubts. In heaven or in hell? Because if his mother was as wicked as Giri says she was to have deserved her destiny, she must be in hell. But this child has not sinned, is not evil. He has probably not even been baptized. So if he dies he will end up in limbo, where all children go who die without being christened. So even then I wouldn't be sending him back to his mother. He sleeps. He trembles a little. But he hates, so it can't be all good, hating is a sin. So that could mean that if I hold this pillow on top of him and show no mercy, it'll be off to hell with his mother, and we'll have given him back and our sinning will be over. And lead us not into temptation. Of course. We were tempted. We fell but we can recover, we can return to grace. But deliver us from evil. Off you go child, off to your mother, waiting for you in one of Satan's cells. I'm sorry, Lord, I know I should not say his name, but my hands are shaking. Thou shalt not kill. Oh. There is also that. But, well, it doesn't say anywhere that we're obliged to give life back once we've taken it away. And I know I will repent for doing this. Yes, Lord. This is the solution. Death will clear me of the sin of theft and confession will wash away the sin of death. Give me strength, Lord, give it to me now. It'll be over in an instant, a moment of breathlessness and it'll all be over.

Maisabé holds the pillow over the sleeping child's face and raises her head to the ceiling. She dreads the baby's convulsions, imagining what they'll feel like; she pictures blood pouring forth, though she only wants to stop it flowing on the inside. The moment of truth arrives and she presses down on the pillow with all her weight, but the baby wriggles to the side and she ends up bashing him with her knuckles. He wakes up startled with a wail. As if by magic, Giri appears in the room and, not understanding what's going on, takes hold of Maisabé by the shoulders and leads her away. She turns around on her way out and the baby, who has stopped crying, looks at Maisabé once more. It is a serious look, of the sort only the very young can have. Amen.

8

Lascano wonders if she will still be there when he gets home. He hopes and fears so and finds himself hesitating in front of the door, looking for his keys that have come off their key ring and have ended up in the depths of his pocket, where the fluff balls accumulate. He slowly puts the key in the lock and opens the door with the care of an unfaithful husband coming home late, *so as not to wake her,* he tells himself, although really he's afraid that he's the one who's dreaming:

Get a grip, Perro, it's half seven in the evening.

The house is dark and silent. Lascano feels relieved but hurt. He's sure she's gone, never to return, that everything will go back to the way it was before, with him all alone, waiting for visits from Marisa's ghost to excite and pain him once again. But then the light comes on and there she is, Eva-Marisa, sitting on the sofa, just as he left her, only now she's wearing his clothes, which are about five sizes too big. She takes his breath away and he lights a cigarette in an unsuccessful attempt to hide his fear and joy. Eva peers at him, like a mouse in a laboratory studies its cage, and is herself surprised by being so pleased to see him, although Lascano doesn't notice this, so busy is he acting casual.

Sorry, I borrowed a few of your clothes. You look like a clown. Well, your wardrobe isn't exactly haute couture, you know. True enough. I was a bit cold.

Perro pauses for a moment. He thinks he's going mad. He doesn't know if he's talking to Marisa or Eva. It's like being trapped in a dream, with no control over his words or actions.

Let's see... I think I've got something that will suit you better.

Lascano goes into his room and shuts the door behind him, without knowing quite why. There's something automatic about his movements. He goes over to his bedside table and rummages around in the drawer. He finds what he's looking for, goes over to the wardrobe, puts a key in the lock and tries to make it turn. The mechanism is stiff from disuse, and it takes a bit of effort before he hears a *clack*, which seems a sinister sound, like a judgement. He takes a deep breath, preparing himself for what's to come. He pulls the doors to the wardrobe wide open. The smell of Marisa, concentrated by the months locked away, rushes upon him like an express train. Lascano holds on tight to the doors so as not to fall to the floor. There in front of him, completely intact, is her whole wardrobe, just as she left it the day she died. He had never before dared open this floodgate. He had never had the courage to face his wife's second skin. He had always looked at this impenetrable place with apprehension, with reverential fear, and now he fights the feeling of having desecrated her tomb. But at the same time, guided by some dark force, he is unable to stop himself. As if having exited his own body, he sees himself on the bed, smoking, and Marisa in front of the mirror, in her underwear, not knowing what to put on, as always, and looking to him, her man, for the necessary approval.

Shall I wear the red dress, do you think? You look nice just as you are. You want me to go out like this? I'd have to call the riot squad. The red dress it is then.

With a beaming smile, Lascano enjoys the spectacle of his wife getting dressed, all the while looking forward to the moment at the end of the night when he will get to undress her.

How do I look?

Lascano, pale as an undertaker, comes out of his room carrying the red dress and gives it to Eva, who murmurs her approval and holds it up to her body. She gracefully spins round and goes into the bathroom. Perro throws himself on the sofa. She soon appears with the dress on. It fits her perfectly.

How do I look?

His whole body screams at him to jump up and tear the dress off, part indignation at this act of usurping, mainly the desperate desire to see her in the full, to taste her, love her, feel her and, more than anything, fuck her. Terror of his own self seizes him: he is not in control of his actions and suddenly the room becomes a trap and he doesn't know what he's capable of. He realizes he has to get out of there immediately, that he cannot remain alone with this woman for another instant, and he stands up abruptly.

I'm hungry. Let's eat out.

Eva picks up on the tension in the air. Everything happened so quickly she didn't even ask herself why this guy had a dress in his room. He's waiting for her by the open door. She puts her shoes on as fast as she can and heads out. As Lascano closes the door, the bird in its cage tweets at him, it is piercing and, this time, incomprehensible.

He walks three paces ahead of Eva. *Is he giving me the chance to escape?* The night starts to get cool and she shivers. Lascano notices and, with all the chivalry of a musketeer from the movies, takes off his jacket and wraps it around her shoulders. She snuggles inside the coat, which smells of him and the Particulares 30 cigarettes he chain-smokes, and she looks at him. He's not very tall, what might be described as normal stature in a country of shorties, but he has broad shoulders. He's yet to develop the pot belly typical of men of his age, nor does he have hairs growing in his ears or nose. He's thinning a little on top, but not too much, and his only grey hairs are the few around his temples, hardly noticeable. He looks quite athletic, which contrasts with the lethargy of his movements. If he were a little more dynamic, he could pass for being ten to fifteen years younger. She stops examining him when their eyes meet, which they do only fleetingly, because he looks away immediately and seems to blush. Although a tough guy clearly lurks behind his cool exterior, she would swear he was scared of her.

They enter a typical neighbourhood bistro and the waiter greets him with some familiarity, as well as no little surprise that he has company. Without even asking her, Lascano orders the daily special for both of them, a jug of house wine and some sparkling water. She tries to comprehend the situation, but doesn't manage in the slightest. When the food arrives, Lascano wolfs his down in four or five mouthfuls, then waits for Eva to finish. When she's halfway through, he begs her pardon and lights a cigarette. He has paid her not the least attention since they sat down and her desire to understand what's happening starts to fade. When she loads the last mouthful onto her fork, Perro asks for the bill. He settles up and they leave. He holds the door for her and as she passes him he makes the most of the moment to gaze at her. The dress looks fantastic on her.

In the cold night air, he feels the whirlwind of his mind calm down and he starts to recover his self-control and he distracts himself thinking about the incredible number of ways women can make themselves look beautiful. Not only can clothing never entirely hide their sexuality, most is designed to emphasize it. These days a woman must try hard to look ugly and really there are no ugly women, only careless ones, and Eva could not look ugly even if she tried, and by then he's had enough of thinking. So he lights a cigarette. Three paces behind him, Eva feels as happy as a little girl on her birthday. She catches up with Lascano, takes him by the arm and holds on to him, in such a way that he feels her breast on his bicep and his sex gets playful and betrays him down in his trousers. Thus they walk the rest of the way home. Lascano doesn't know whether he wants her to let go of him or for the journey to last for ever. She hums softly and now even rests her head upon his shoulder. Her pheromone-charged scent attacks Perro. His body feels the physical need for this other body with an intensity beyond any thought and he clenches his fists in his pockets to prevent himself jumping on her right there and then. But they've reached the narrow doorway of his building and they have to separate to get through.

Outside the apartment, Eva leans against the wall and looks at him as he searches for his keys, but she doesn't look at him in any old way. Her eyes are full of provocation, her pupils fearless, her breasts rise and fall to the rhythm of her breathing. He opens the door and looks at her arse as she walks into the flat. She knows he's looking, and he knows that she knows, and he asks himself how is it that a woman can tell when you're looking at her arse. And he hears, or thinks he hears, the sad bolero about lost lovers. And she sees him cross the room and plunge into his bedroom, shutting the door behind him, and she doesn't hear him cry because he cries in silence, but he does cry. He sleeps in his clothes. Tonight Marisa doesn't come to visit him. Cross with him, no doubt. But when he sleeps:

I am in the desert. It's night-time. The immense sense of isolation is like being at sea. It's alive, more than present. It's everything. It surrounds me and drowns me. The desert and I start to become one being. It gets inside me. I am seated, trying to bore through the darkness and, finally, the desert is a mirror in which I see every person I've ever known. Very clear and distinct. All the emotions I've ever experienced come to me, one after the other, with no respite, while the moon tears apart the night like a barracuda does a fish. Alchemy, transmutation: I am the desert and the desert is me. And suddenly I am howling at that very moon. Outside, the sun glares and filters its rays with fury into the room where I think I'm a horse, a fox, a bat. I ask myself: What are you? Are you a horse, a fox or a mouse?

He wakes up, drowning in his own sweat. He gets up, stumbles out of the room. On the sofa Eva sleeps. She has carefully folded up her new clothes and neatly placed them on a chair. A long arm dangles out of the blanket. He moves closer, gently touches her hand. Only to assure himself that she's not part of the dream, of the desert, that she is really there, alive. She is there.

9

One o'clock. Florida high street. Hustle and bustle. The galloping inflation unleashed upon 1979 infects everyone. Office workers, financial traders and beggars alike are all prey to the frenetic uncertainty. Those with money rush to spend it, for soon it will not be worth the paper it's printed on. Those without money will never have any.

Although winter chills prevail, as the elderly are only too aware, there's a feeling, but only a feeling, of spring in the air. Not for Amancio, though, who is buried up to his eyeballs in debt. What really worries him is his debt with Biterman: the Jew could lift the lid on his financial shenanigans at any moment. Amancio has fraudulently guaranteed several different loans against the same assets, each time craftily hiding his outstanding obligations. So the cheques he signed for Biterman could prove to be the straw that breaks the camel's back. Everything else he signed can only lead to civil court orders, which drag on at their own slow pace and can take up to ten years to resolve with the right delaying tactics, and even then there's a strong chance that the whole matter will come to nothing. But the cheques can send him straight to a penal court. If

Biterman decides to declare him bankrupt, the whole pack of creditors will set upon him. This in turn will bring about his total ruin and, most probably, send him to Devoto jail. Amancio wakes up punctually at five o'clock every morning imagining such a scenario in a panic of fear and revulsion. The Jew has to be stopped in his tracks somehow and a brilliant idea as to how suddenly comes to Amancio: Giribaldi.

Throughout his youth, in his free time between Military College, his activities with the Tacuara far-right movement, Father Meinvielle's anti-semitic lectures at the Huemul bookshop and Sunday mass, Giri played scrum-half for Atalya, with Amancio a three-quarter. They became friends over post-match beers, visits to brothels in Carupá, parties at the Atlético de San Isidro rugby club or the Rowing Club, where these young rabble-rousers, smoking and dressed in tuxedos, stood around flexing their muscles. The girls from the Jesús María, Anunciata and Malinkrodt convent schools loved to lead the lads on, but were instinctively repulsed by the idea of taking things further. Thus the boys left the parties horny and smarting, spilling onto the street as a gang ready for a fight. They would look for one, and find one: there was always some unsuspecting idiot to take their frustration out on, burn off some of the testosterone the girls had brought to the boil. Naturally, Giri was mob leader. Nobody had asked him to be, he just assumed the role by being the biggest and cruellest lout of them all, and because no one in the group dared stand up to him. Whenever anyone protested, Giri would stop him dead with his steely stare, enough to remind any upstart how brutally he dealt with street-fight victims.

Giri had calmed down these days, a married man and an officer of the Argentine Army, deeply committed to the fight against the vague generic term of "subversion". His stories of extracting confessions via electric shock, of executing communists, of all his repression exploits, had in Amancio their only confidant.

Making out like he'd rather not be bringing the matter up but using their binding friendship as cover, Amancio plans to ask Giri's advice on what to do about his debts with Biterman. He really hopes that Giri will do him the favour of making the problem go away. After all, Jews and communists go together hand in hand, and Giri professes to hate the Sons of Israel even more than he does the followers of Lenin. Giribaldi has the means and the power to make Biterman disappear for ever, and Amancio's main worries along with him. With this in mind, Amancio walks along Florida, carrying the world on his shoulders. He heads towards Augustus where, over a coffee, he daydreams about the Jew being crossed off his list of problems.

A coffee with cream please, kid. How you doing, Giri? Really awful. Maisabé's gone mad. I don't know what the hell's up with her. Why? Well, you know how she always wanted a kid. But unfortunately… she can't. We've tried everything. Nothing doing. She did get pregnant once, but soon lost it. A miscarriage. But I thought you were going to adopt? Well, that's just the thing. A week ago I brought her a baby. Fair hair, healthy, beautiful. But it brings her out in a fit; she looks at it as if it's a monster. She's scared of it, and has started saying and doing strange things. Like what? I don't know. All that nonsense about God and the Devil. She wants to know who its parents are, where they are. I don't get it. Basically, she's been going on and on about wanting a fucking child and now that

71

she has one she cries all day and all night. Last night I found her by the cot. The kid was bawling like a pig and she was standing there, at its side, frozen stiff, as if hypnotized. Tell me something, does anyone really understand women? They don't even know what the bloody hell they want themselves. I had to give her a slap to bring her back to her senses. She's making me ill is what she's doing. Look, the main thing is for you to calm down. Women are like that. All of them. No prick is ever good enough for them. She spends the whole time banging on about guilt and sin. OK, I've an idea. Let's hope it's a good one. There's a guy at San Martín who attended Military College with me for a while, until he discovered his true vocation and became a priest. His name's Roberto, go see him and tell him I sent you. He's helpful, understands things. You can tell him everything and he'll give you some good advice. What Maisabé needs is for someone with authority to bless the child. You'll see then how the whole thing resolves itself. You reckon? Count on it. And where do I find this priest? I'll give you the address later. Don't forget. While you're here though, there's a problem I wanted to ask you about. Go on. Well, you know that I've been going about cap in hand for a while. Haven't we all. Your problem is you spend what you haven't got trying to keep Lara satisfied. And she's never satisfied with anything, of course. Look, are you going to hear me out or give me a lecture? Fine, go on. Well, I've ended up scrounging off some Jew in Once and now he's squeezing me. What have you signed? Some cheques. A stack this high. And has he tried to cash them? Yeah, and the bank bounced them. And so? Now he's given me a deadline to pay him by, otherwise I have to hand over the ranch or he sends me to jail. Threaten him and get the cheques back off him. You reckon? These Yids are all cowards. Have you got a gun? I've got the nine you gave me for my birthday. Go over and point that at his head. You'll see how fast he coughs up the *cheques. And what if he kicks up a fuss? What fuss is he going to kick up? I'm telling you, these fucking Jews, all bark but no bite. When the shit comes home to roost, they turn chicken. If you do have any problems, call me and then we'll see. OK. You scratch my back and I'll scratch yours. Don't forget to give me the address of that priest. I've got to sort this mess out with Maisabé once and for all. I'll give it to you later. Right, I'm off, you take care of the coffees, OK? Have I got any choice?*

10

Sitting in the dark, Eva asks herself: *What is it he wants?* Everyone wants something. She decides she'll start probing Lascano. *Let's find out what he's up to and see if we can't engineer a safe way out of here,* she's thinking to herself when Perro arrives home. He switches on the light and takes off his coat. She looks beautiful yet distant, staring at some undefined point on the wall,

Is anything wrong? No. I just got the feeling there might be something the matter. Is this an interrogation? I was only asking. And what does it matter to you whether I'm OK or not? Well, it's not so much that it matters to me... Well, if it doesn't matter to you, then why have you got me held prisoner here? What do you mean? Every time you go out, you lock me in. Do you want to go out, do you want to leave? I want to know what you want from me. Look, girl... The name's Eva. Sorry, Eva. I don't want anything from you. I'm your own private prisoner then, is that it? I'm not in the habit of having prisoners in my own home. Oh, no? Where do you usually dump them then? I don't dump them anywhere, I hand them over to the judge. Don't give me that, we all know what coppers get up to. Oh really, and what's that then? Like you don't know. Look, girl... sorry, Eva. I try to stick to the law. Oh, fuck off. What law would that be then? There are laws; what's missing is justice.

And who do you think you are, the Lone Ranger? I don't think I'm anybody. All I know is that I have my work to do and I try to do it as best I can. And since when did cops do any work? Personally, I've worked since the age of fifteen, and you? And me what? Nothing. The mysterious superintendent. What have I done to annoy you so much? I want to know what you want with me. I'm protecting you. Don't ask me why. Protecting me. You want me to suck you off? OK. I'll suck you off. You want to fuck me? OK, fuck me... I don't want anything. Don't make me laugh. You'd be the first cop... That's enough, you want to leave? You know where the door is.

Eva gets up and heads determinedly for the door.

I'm sorry... Sorry for what? I didn't realize. Didn't realize what? That I locked you in. It's habit. I'm always forgetting my keys, so I make sure I lock the door properly when I leave so as to remind myself to take them. What? If I always have to lock the door when I go out, then I can't forget my keys. I've lived alone for a long time. Whatever, I'm off. Please yourself. But without a cent and with no documentation I doubt you'll get far. The military are very active in the streets these days. That's my problem. True enough. Well then, I'm off. Off you go then.

Lascano watches her leave with mixed emotions: relieved to recover his solitude, anguished already by her absence. He starts to follow her, but changes his mind, stops and lights a cigarette.

Out of the womb, everything is exposed to the world. The street seems sinister to Eva. Beneath her summer dress, she feels the cold between her legs and she shivers. She comes across a few coins in a pocket. Finding a public telephone that works these days can be a real feat. Eva is lucky, but her calls come to nothing, or worse. An unfamiliar male voice answers Domingo's number. Eva gives her password, but he replies with any old thing. She hangs up. Either Domingo's been caught or he's on the run. Her second call goes unanswered. The third is met by a female voice:

We've just arrived. Who's that?

The response is supposed to be: *Was flight 505 on time?* Eva hangs up. There's no one left to turn to. The cell has been disbanded. Right now, those who've been captured and illegally detained will be trying to get through the first twenty-four hours of torture without speaking. That was deemed sufficient time for comrades to spread the word and disappear, before someone else makes them disappear for good. The military knows this and the race against the clock makes them ever more savage.

Night draws in and promises rain. The streets are deserted. Eva has to turn back quickly as she reaches the main road, burying herself in the dark shadows of the plantain trees on the side street. At the corner, two Falcons pass by, full of gorillas, the barrels of their Ithacas poking out the windows. They're on her trail, and anybody else's. It's hunting hour and she's among the prey. Unarmed, she feels naked. She trips on a loose paving stone and splashes dirty water up her legs. It seems like a sign. She walks for blocks and blocks, in tears, the cold of the night biting at her wet cheeks, her body begging for respite. She has nowhere to go, but pride stops her from returning to Lascano's. Though hardly ideal, it is her only possible refuge. When she accepts this, she starts to make her way back. When she gets to his building, she hesitates, desperately going over her options one more time, but there are none.

The light in the entrance hall suddenly comes on and a teenage boy steps out of the lift. Eva pretends to be looking for her keys as he comes out of the door and he holds it open for her. Inside, the cold immediately relaxes its grip and there's a delicious smell floating down the stairs of home-cooked beef escalopes with garlic and parsley. Her tummy rumbles. Outside Lascano's door, she hesitates again, but only briefly, because there are people coming and going. Ignoring the bell, she taps lightly on the wood three times. Part of her wants Lascano not to hear, but he's been leaning against the door since she left, smoking one cigarette after another, thinking about her, and so his body feels the knocking before his ears hear it. He opens the door as if he's been expecting her all along. The sky provides the special effects, thunder, lightning and the sort of torrential downpour more typical of a hot summer's day.

Fancy seeing you here? Forgive me, I'm just a silly little girl. Let's not kid ourselves. We both know the streets are mean. Can I stay here until I get my papers and some money together? Those who go without being asked to leave can return without invitation. So I can stay then? Under one condition. I thought there would be. Tonight, you cook. You sure like living dangerously. Is your cooking really that bad? To be honest, I can't even fry an egg. OK then, I'll make you an offer: I'll teach you. Really? I'm starving, so let's get started right away. I'm raring to go. Today's class, my speciality, pasta with tomato sauce. Again? Again. The first lesson is this: to cook well you have to cook with pleasure, otherwise the food turns out bad. My grandma used to say you had to cook with love. Well, it's the same thing, and cooking and loving have several things in common, not least their unpleasant side. Meaning? Tears. And so, chopping the onion is your job. Ah, so I get the worst job. The apprentice always gets the worst job. Yes, sir, superintendent, sir! Stop playing the fool and get chopping. And very finely... Whatever you say. Now this bit's very important: so that the sauce doesn't go all acidic, you have to add some sugar to the tomatoes. Like this? Perfect. Do you like garlic? I love it. Excellent. I don't trust people who don't like garlic. You don't say. You're a little odd, hey? Very odd. Now cut this clove of garlic into tiny little pieces... You see that little green root inside? That? Yes. Take it out. Sometimes it can be very bitter...

In the confined space of the kitchen, Eva and Lascano relax in each other's company, concentrating on the task in hand and drawing close enough to smell one another. As the food takes shape, they can't help brushing into each other from time to time, and can't help liking it when it happens amid the aroma of frying onion and garlic. The kitchen heats up like a furnace and their body temperatures rise accordingly, warming to the domestic harmony. There are patches of sky where life can be forgotten, the bleakness suspended, while, inside, a juicy pepper, red as blood, yields under Lascano's knife, ready to incite the mixture simmering away in the frying pan. The pot of hot water bubbles and impatiently demands spaghetti. The onions sting Eva's eyes and surprise her with a feeling of remorse, but her need for a sense of home and a little good cheer is greater, and so for the moment she files away her pain, her fear, her constant state of being on guard. She grabs the bottle of wine Lascano has used to spice up the sauce, pours two glasses and they toast in the proper fashion, looking each other in the eye. Her body burns. Lascano feels a shiver, like that of the male spider entering the black widow's web.

11

Amancio has the distinct feeling his life is tumbling down around him. Even so, he's sometimes overcome by a crazy kind of certainty that everything is about to change for the better. This sudden optimism never arises from him doing something concrete to improve his financial circumstances – it's all he can do to keep himself afloat – rather he imagines that a miracle is about to occur. He daydreams that he witnesses a hold-up and that in the shoot out the thief falls dead at his feet with a briefcase. Amancio picks it up and somehow contrives to slip away from the police and when he opens the valise, there's a million dollars inside. Or he gets into a lift with another man carrying a briefcase. It's just the two of them. The other guy has a fit, a heart attack or something, and falls down unconscious on the floor. Amancio checks that the guy is out cold and takes off with the attaché and when he opens it, there's a million dollars inside. But now is not really the time for such fantasizing and so he stands up, straightens his trousers, looks at himself in the mirror and leaves the bathroom without flushing the toilet, something that drives Lara mad.

You always forget, Amancio, always. We're going to have to transplant an eye into your arse so you can see the shit for yourself.

Lara finishes rinsing off under the shower. Amancio spies

on her from the shadows of the corridor, thinking she doesn't notice. Even wearing the ridiculous plastic shower cap, she looks amazing. Lara could dress in rags and her beauty wouldn't be diminished in the slightest. In fact, it would stand out all the more for the contrast. She turns off the taps, takes off the shower cap and shakes her hair in a circular motion, which fascinates Amancio even more.

It's getting late. The party never starts until I get there. Madam is too modest. It's true. Nothing happens when it's just the die-hard Jockey Club regulars. Pass me my dressing gown.

Lara lets him put the garment over her shoulders, but when he moves to embrace her, she slips away with a calculated, agile movement, proving once again that she's one step ahead of him. In the bedroom she sits in front of the mirror and brushes her hair, like a femme fatale from a white telephone movie, admiring herself all the while. There's much to admire.

Amancio, why don't you make us a drink?

She's not sure she fancies a drink, but she certainly doesn't fancy giving Amancio the pleasure of staring at her naked body and, at the same time, she saves herself the bother of having to reject him when he starts his annoying advances. She quickly puts on her underwear. Provocative, yes, easy, never, or at least not now, not with this fool. When Amancio gets back, jingling the ice in the glasses like some hotshot, Lara is already putting her black dress on, a garment which set him back the price of five Hereford cows when he bought it for her in Paris. This dress, like a starry night sky painted onto Lara's body, is proof manifest of the curvature of space.

What are we going to do? We're going to the party at the Jockey Club. That much I know. Then I don't understand the question. I'm asking about our winter holiday. I don't know, go out to the ranch? The countryside bores me, Amancio, can't you come up with anything better? Like what? Like a trip. We haven't been anywhere for over a year. Well, where would you like to go? Ibiza wouldn't be a bad option. We're not really in a position to be going to Ibiza at the moment, my dear. It seems like you're not in a position to be going on a day trip to Chascomús lake.

As Amancio walks away from the discussion, Lara takes a good swig from her glass and pulls a face at him in the mirror.

Pérez Lastra goes over to his forlorn-looking gun rack. All he's got left is the Sauer 12 gauge shotgun, which he inherited from his father, and the nine millimetre which Giribaldi gave him for his birthday. The Remington, the Winchester, the Skorpio with the added double barrel and all the rest ended up at the Banco Municipal de Préstamos, the state-owned pawnbroker, the intention always being to recover them before the expiry date of the tickets. But neither thief nor businessman appeared with the million-dollar suitcase and so the guns never came home, instead ending up under the ruthless hammer of the auctioneer and in the hands of strangers. Amancio curses his luck. He moves away from the display case feeling dazed and calls to Lara from the corridor that he'll wait for her down in the car. Lara makes another funny face, a second swig of her drink having put a twinkle in her eye and got her in a party mood. If she wants to enjoy herself tonight, she knows she'll have to shackle Amancio somehow.

Down on the street, making her way to the car, Lara has to dodge past a rubbish truck and inspires the admiration of the filthy, rough, brawny workers.

Hey girl, with an arse as sweet as that you must shit bon-bons.

Amancio hears the lewd remark and makes a motion as if to get out of the car. Lara intercepts him.

Calm down baby, I don't want to spend the night at the hospital.

The journey is short and silent. Lara sits sulking, head turned to the window.

Are you in a bad mood? What I am is fed up. Fed up with what? Don't act the idiot, Amancio, you know very well what I'm fed up with. Everything will be sorted out soon. Change the record, this one broke way back. You take everything too seriously. Well, you never do anything to improve things. Everything is a problem to you. Oh I'm sorry, I was forgetting, sir hasn't a problem in the world. I've got something lined up that's going to sort everything out. Well, I sure hope it's not another one of your fantasies. This time I'd better see results. Go and kill yourself, you damn idiot. Are you listening to me? You'd better come up with some results. With your help I'll come up with plenty. What did you just say? Nothing, I didn't say anything. I'm sick of your mumbling. Don't be like that, I was only singing. You'll be singing to Gardel soon, the rate you're going. Oh, don't talk rubbish.

The salon is full of the well-to-do. Everyone is very elegant, the gentlemen in tuxedos, the ladies in evening gowns. Mixed among the civilian wardrobes are a handful of military men, dressed in their forces finery, from colonel upwards. Lara and Amancio sit at their adorned table in silence. Amancio put Horacio on the guest list to impress him, and hoped through him to gain favour with Biterman, thereby extending his payments deadline, and maybe even the credit line. When Amancio invited him, Horacio jumped for joy: he'd always dreamed of setting foot in the salons where the bourgeois progeny congregate. And here he comes, his red hair floating above the crowd, as he athletically winds his way through the well-developed paunches of the landholding class. Amancio gets to his feet to greet him.

How are you, buddy, how are you? Come on, sit down. Allow me to introduce you to my wife, Lara. Delighted. Your husband described you to me, but it seems he came up short. Amancio always comes up short. Lara! It was a joke, silly. Will you pour us some champagne? Of course. OK then, a toast. What shall we drink to? I can think of nothing more deserving of a toast than you, Lara. Your friend's very charming, Amancio, you've kept him well hidden. You'll have to come and see us more often. I'd be glad to.

Lara looks carefully at Horacio. What he interprets as polite feminine interest is in fact the quick radiography she performs on any man who crosses her path. The verdict: clearly a loser, like her husband, but a fine young man nevertheless, with a pianist's hands. A roll in the hay is not out of the question. Looking over the heads of the two men keeping her company, Lara's face suddenly lights up. She has spotted Ramiro, a half-cousin and occasional lover, ever the charmer, always elegant and always extremely rich in every sense. Ramiro comes up to Amancio from behind and slaps him on the back, a bit too hard.

Well, if it isn't the Pérez Lastras. How's it going, buddy?

There's nothing worse than Ramiro as far as Amancio's concerned. Even as a child, Ramiro would slight him, and although Amancio is ten years older, he has never managed to beat Ramiro at anything; Ramiro is an excellent sportsman. Amancio feels all the old animosity swell up inside him as Ramiro kisses Lara on both cheeks, the French way, doing so too close to the mouth, and lingering too long.

Lara, every day plus adorable. *And you look younger by the day. What's your secret? The good life is my secret. Doing whatever one wants, whenever one wants and with whomever one wants.*

Noticing Horacio's presence, Ramiro extends a hand and a broad smile.

Ramiro Elicetche Barroetaveña, a pleasure to meet you. Horacio Biterman, delighted. Biterman... With one n or two? With one... OK, if you gents don't mind, Lara, would you do me the honour of a dance? I'd love to.

Amancio watches them move away towards the dance floor, hand in hand, whispering and giggling to one another. He starts to stew with anger, but Horacio snaps him out of it, nodding in Lara's direction.

Congratulations. Thanks. Although sometimes... Sometimes what? Well, being with such a good-looking young woman is sometimes like doing your military service. You have to be on your guard, hang on her every whim, put up with her comings and goings. I imagine it has its compensations. It does, but less often than you might like to imagine. I'm telling you, man, all women are the same, young or old, they're forever getting headaches, feeling out of sorts or whatever the excuse may be. Always the same old story. A girl I know maintains that women don't actually like fucking. Oh I think they like it, but they don't like that they like it. Now tell me, given that you're old, ugly and poor, how on earth did you pull a beauty like that? With patience, dear boy, lots of patience. Anyway, let's talk business: I don't know what to do about your brother. Didn't you manage to sort anything out with him? No chance. Your big brother, my friend, is impossible. Now he's got it into his head that he wants everything I owe him all in one go. He's putting the squeeze on is he? Squeezing me like an orange. I told him I can't wring water from a stone. But he got all unreasonable. I don't know what's the matter with him lately. He's more miserable than ever. The truth is he made me want to smash his face against the wall. I often feel that way too. I can't believe you're brothers. You're so different. We've always been that way. He loves money above everything else. I love life. He lives only to scrimp and scrape. I don't know how to handle him. Now he's set on

*taking La Rencorosa from me. If he does that, it's all over for me. If
he takes up his claim, the whole tribe will be upon me... It does seem
like he's got his eye on the country pad. A friend of mine reckons I
should just go and force him to give me the cheques back. What, play
the tough guy? Yes, threaten him, he reckons Elías is a chicken. Does
he know him? No. So what makes him think that? I don't know, he
just said it sounded like he was from the way I described him.*

What's being said between the lines hits Horacio like
a kick between the legs: *Jews are cowards.* He heard it
hundreds of times at school. A spiteful, contemptuous
knot tightens inside him: *if this idiot only knew.* His brother's
story, and the few times he has seen Elías angry, is enough
to inspire complete terror in Horacio. Beneath the surface
of the prudent, calculating moneylender lies a beast
ready to attack. A resolute man who has killed before
and is prepared to do so again, and Amancio thinks he
could easily give him a fright. If Horacio were to persuade
Amancio to go and threaten Elías, one of them would
inevitably end up dead. If his brother were killed, Horacio
would be his only heir. If Amancio were killed, it'd be no
great loss to the world. The risk was that something could
go wrong and Horacio's complicity in the plan would be
revealed, although it could always be denied. It was far
more likely that as soon as Amancio threatened him, Elías
would pounce; Amancio would then be left with no option
but to shoot him. In any case, it was only like putting a
chip on the number five: if the five comes up then great,
but if not, things would be no worse than they are now. *The
reward's worth the risk,* he concludes.

*Well, it's not a bad idea, but you'd have to give him one hell
of a scare to make him give up. How? Look, Elías is terrified of
guns, it's something left over from the war. And so? Have you got
a pistol? Yes. Go pay him a visit and point the gun at him. I split*

at seven. So if you arrive after that, you'll catch him alone and I won't feel obliged to intervene. You reckon? Look, I've a better idea. So that you take him completely by surprise, I'll give you my key. You sneak in without making a sound and give him the fright of his life. You'll see how he backs down. And what if he doesn't? He's my brother, I know what he's like. And what if he goes mad? Well, you'll be armed. Hey, mate, what are you saying? Just a word to the wise. Have you gone crazy? You're the one who's crazy if you think you can talk him round with pleasantries. He's going to ruin you. I'm telling you. But, you do realize what you're saying? If, in the worst case scenario, Elías dies, it solves all your problems, and mine too. I don't know, mate, it seems a bit...

Pam, pam, papám. The dancing suddenly stops and, as if by some collective Pavlovian reflex, everyone stands up. A solemn mood descends upon the entire crowd at the sound of the first chords of the national anthem. The military men stand to attention and flaunt their patriotism with their intense salutes. At the opening line calling for all mortals to hear, *oíd mortales,* someone pipes up with a pretentious baritone. Lara and Ramiro make the most of the distraction to place themselves as far away as possible from the dance floor, out of sight from Amancio. Horacio, meanwhile, becomes completely distracted by someone to his right. The patriotic homage ends with repeated pledges to die for the glory of the nation, *juremos con gloria morir,* and then there's a din of chairs being rearranged until the chaos of laughter and voices returns. The sighting of potential prey has awoken Horacio's predatory instinct.

Have you seen who's over here? Who? Quiroga, I've been hungering after her for ages. Excuse me a moment. Go for it.

Horacio heads over to Isondú Quiroga, a fine young example of provincial nobility, three time "Miss Yerba Mate" and daughter of the biggest *mate* producer in

Misiones province. She is as much a lady as she is a wild animal, her eyes glowing like hot coals on her olive skin. *She's good enough to eat*, thinks Horacio, as he sits down beside her smiling face. Amancio, with no little envy eating away at his soul, is left alone at the table, feeling pensive. He remembers Lara. His gaze searches the room for her in vain; they've disappeared. He serves himself a glass of champagne and pours it down his throat. He gets up, walks around the place looking for her, checks all the adjoining salons, but to no avail, so he returns to the table and sits down again. An hour goes by, two, the occasional acquaintance comes over to speak to him, but his eyes never stop looking for Lara. Another hour passes and the guests start to drift off, the party enters its death throes. Amancio has not stopped drinking or seeking out Lara, but his senses start to betray him. Horacio comes over to bid him farewell and whispers in his ear.

What we spoke of earlier. If you decide to go for it, this is the key for downstairs, this one for upstairs. Tomorrow he'll be there until late. Think about it. Give my love to the bombshell.

...and he leaves, arm round Isondú's waist. Amancio holds the keys as if they're a lucky charm. When he's finally convinced that Lara's not coming back, he puts the keys in his pocket, gets up and leaves. Outside on the street, he realizes he's too drunk to drive and so takes a taxi home. Amancio's head is a maelstrom. Horacio has told him to kill his brother if necessary. Elías's death would indeed be the best solution to his problems. But he's not sure he's really up for killing a guy. *Give him a fright, yes, but kill him?* The image of Biterman's dead body pops into Amancio's head and it repulses him. He has heard Giribaldi say that many people shit themselves at the moment of death. *If giving him a real fright doesn't work then I can always ask Giri to take care of the Yid. After all, what difference does one more death make to him?*

Dawn breaks. Amancio, in his dishevelled tuxedo, is asleep on the living-room sofa. And he carries on sleeping until almost seven in the evening, when the sound of the door shocks him awake. Lara arrives home, worn out.

Madam returns. Oh Amancio, don't start. Do you want to tell me where the hell you've been? Don't remind me or I'll go back there. You've been out all night and all day, would you care to explain to me what happened? Nothing happened. What could happen? Ramiro invited us to his yacht, and you know how it is, time flies when you're having fun... Of course, someone's wife disappearing for a whole day is just such marvellous fun. Don't upset yourself Amancio, your blood pressure will rise and you've got enough problems. Whereas you don't appear to have a care in the world. Does it not seem a bit humiliating to you that you barefacedly flirt in front of me and then disappear leaving me sitting there in front of everyone? Don't talk rubbish. Rubbish? You were born a whore and you'll die a whore. Well at least I know what I am. You're a whore and you don't even realize it. What did you just say? Ten thousand. What? I said ten thousand. What are you talking about? How much you slipped out of my purse the other night. I don't know what you're talking about. Look, I might have been asleep, but I wasn't in a coma. I went to bed with thirty thousand in my purse and got up with twenty. And you think I need to swipe ten thousand off you? Last time it was five. Stop your bullshit. You'd best come up with something very soon. I'm not going to put up with this much longer. You're the one who has to get his act together, or are you not the man of this affair? Am I making myself clear? All you care about is money. My mother taught me one thing: he who undresses me, clothes me. And don't come to me with that country values nonsense, dear. Deep down, you're just a common pimp. Well, everyone gets what they deserve. You might have fooled me with the lord of the manor act but the mask has long since slipped. I'm warning you, your days are numbered. Either you improve things for me or you won't be seeing me any more. Like that is it? As simple as.

Lara disappears into the bedroom leaving Amancio to chew on his fury and helplessness. He pours himself a glass of Tres Plumas whisky and throws it down in one swig, but his stomach rejects it and he has to go running to the toilet in the spare bathroom and vomit, hugging the porcelain until he's reduced to a few dry and painful retches. When he can finally get up, he returns to the living room and slumps back on the sofa. Around eleven at night, he stirs to see Lara about to walk out the door again.

What are you doing, where are you going? I'm going out to meet one of the girls for a coffee, you got a problem with that? Because if you do, there's the door, feel free to leave. The door is there for you too, Lara. Yeah, but I'm the one who pays the rent. Which means it's your way out. Enough is enough, Lara. That's what I've been saying. Enough fighting I mean, I don't want to fight with you. That's fine by me. Don't be so pessimistic. I've enough stress as it is, so don't go on at me any more. I've always funded us, have done for a long time, wouldn't you say? So have a little more faith in me. I'll give you all the faith you want. But faith is not going to pay the bills, and I feel enough of a prize fool as it is. I'll have everything fixed soon, you'll see. You better had do.

Devastated and confused, Amancio hears the lift door open and close, the distant sound of its motor up in the dark roof. Like a lightning bolt, he's struck with the idea that she has gone to meet Horacio. Although no, they never had a chance to arrange it. At no point were they ever alone together. But their exchange of eager looks didn't go unnoticed. Amancio is in love with Lara, in it up to his neck. He knows, feels she's more than he deserves.

The story about meeting up with one of the girls doesn't fool him for a second. It'll be Ramiro or else her boss, the Pole with the name with more consonants than vowels. And he can do nothing to stop her, nor can he stop the blood rushing to his head, the choking in his chest. He has no power of control over Lara, no influence, nothing he can offer to keep her sweet. She has given him an ultimatum and the clock is ticking.

He goes to the mini bar, serves himself a Tres Plumas and necks it. The drink is like a bag of rabid cats tumbling down his throat. He sinks another shot to drown them, then another, and another. Finally he starts to calm down and the image of a naked Lara on top of the naked Pole fades away and loses importance. His body has cooled down, the pain numbed, the hatred frozen. After the fifth or sixth shot, he smashes the empty bottle on the floor and he thinks that Biterman, the Jews and the Poles of the world are to blame for his predicament. He goes over to the display cabinet with a stupid smile on his lips. He opens the case, takes out the nine millimetre. He caresses it. The gun's as cold as he is. He opens the box of steel-tipped bullets. He removes the magazine, fills it with the eight cartridges, one by one, and tucks the pistol in his belt. One lonely bullet is left in the box and he pops it in his pocket. He goes into the bedroom, takes out his tweed blazer, looking somewhat worn on the lapels, and puts it on. He straightens his tie, resplendent with crests, and leaves.

Time to teach that fucking Jew a few home truths.

When the lift doors open and close and he hears the motor upstairs, it feels good that he too is going out and he thinks that everything is about to change. That it is the Jew who has brought him all his bad luck. He feels in control of the situation.

12

Manuel felt like a prisoner trapped in his own body. Always on the move, as if trying to escape from his own skin. Always running, always fleeing, always thirsty, always out front, always crossing roads without looking. Eva spent the entire day thinking about Manuel. Their non-future together. Living a clandestine existence has the destructive side-effect of giving everything a temporary nature, unstable and blurred. They first got together after the demonstration outside the Ministry of Social Welfare, when two hundred thousand voices had chanted in unison that José López Rega had been born to a whore: *López Ré / López Ré / López Rega / la puta que te parió*. The passions aroused in them that day never developed into true love, if such a thing even exists. The cause was always more important, the future but a suspended execution sentence. Manuel would never be the father of her child. His death was no more than a confirmation of this certainty. Their assignments kept them apart and they separately went about their tasks with total conviction, intent on changing the world by force, whether the world wanted it or not. They were part of a youth movement violently indoctrinated by the words of the new prophets, like Che Guevara, who during their brief lives appealed to them with pompous pronouncements: *Let me tell you, at the risk of sounding ridiculous, that the true guerrillero is guided by deep feelings of love.* Death and sex, always getting mixed up together, combined in Eva and Manuel in uneven measures. The result was a lethal cocktail. That last time he inhabited her body, quickly, like in a dream, in a rush, in the hideout in Villa Martelli, she didn't even get as far as orgasm, never mind making him understand she was late, telling him her dream, her pressing need to abandon the armed struggle.

Eva doesn't want to die, doesn't want them to kill what's growing inside her, the child her body tells her is there more clearly than any medical examination could ever do. She's glad they didn't capture Manuel alive, that he died in combat and thus avoided the beatings and execution simulations, was spared being tied to a bed and electrocuted, having his head submerged in water over and over again. She hates herself for having this as her only comfort and she hates him for having sacrificed himself. And dead he may be, but she can't forgive him for not having realized what he was, the father of her child, for not having been closer. A line from the play, *Yerma*, suddenly resonates with her. She remembers seeing Nuria Espert's performance at a theatre on Corrientes Avenue, her words full of yearning for something she knew she would never have, as she asked her pregnant neighbour:

What does it feel like to be pregnant? Have you ever held a live bird in your hand? It's like that, only in your blood.

The world seems more distant to Eva today, and she seems less responsible for it. She just wants to live and she dreams of the moment when she puts her breasts, already bulging out of her bra, into the mouth of the child who floats inside her, who knows nothing of the stupidity of men. She feels a sudden need, overwhelming and urgent, to be hugged. But she's alone in this strange house. She could easily escape if she wanted to, but she doesn't want to, she wants to stay as she is, lying on the sofa, watching the hours pass by, rejoicing in the silence, or at least the muffling of the row of the outside world. She just wants to be left to brood, to cackle with laughter one minute, cry the next. Her skin has gotten smoother, softer, her hair more shiny. She imagines a girl. Plaiting her hair ready for school, *in case of lice...* She imagines a boy in the park with a red ball. *I might not have managed to make the world a better place for everyone, but I'll make sure it's better for my son.* But she thinks, she remembers:

...I am in blood. Stepp'd in so far that, should I wade no more, returning were as tedious as go o'er...

...and she knows there's no turning back, she can't become unpregnant, nor does she want to, and she's afraid. It seems clear to her that there are two kinds of coward: those who beat a retreat and those who make a break for it. The moment has come for her to plan her escape, because she's become surrounded. She can almost hear the barking of the dictatorship's dogs with their slobbering tongues, sniffing out the streets in search of her. They can smell her sweat, her pregnant female scent. She chases such thoughts away, determined not to let them take hold inside her. She would like to go back to being a little girl, feel herself protected, free of these worries, and she dreams of a different country, dreams of the sea and starts to organize her thoughts of exile:

On balance: I'm alive. This refuge is perfect for the moment. I'm in the house of a cop who doesn't ask questions and who intrigues me, what does he want from me? He says he wants to help me. The three things I need start with "D": dough, documents, disguise. Let's see where we stand. There are the two wads of dollar bills that Tony Ventura left hidden in the brothel, which must still be there and that Lascano didn't see. I have to find a way of getting them. I can't just rock up at the house and tell the concierge I've come to collect something I left behind. In any case, I don't even dare leave the house on my own at the moment. I'll have to find a way to get Lascano to take me there. Documents. He can help me with those too, as the police produce more false documents than anyone, but how can I ask him without giving myself away? The disguise is the easy part. If I wear the beige fitted suit that's in the closet, even if it is really for summer, and put my hair in a bun, I could easily pass for a well-to-do lady from Barrio Norte. So I'll have to get to work on Lascano, study his movements. He behaves towards me with such a strange mixture of admiration and terror. What's up with the guy? When he found me, it was as if he'd seen a ghost. What's going on? I need to find out more.

Eva stands up, goes into the kitchen and makes herself a cup of tea. Cup in hand, she takes tiny sips of the still bubbling hot liquid, enjoying tormenting her tongue as she used to do as a little girl, and walks around the house. She goes into the bedroom and opens drawers, making sure everything is put back in its precise place. Underpants, socks, shirts, handkerchiefs, ties. The drawer on the bedside table is lined with oilskin. It's full of empty packets of cigarettes, papers, used pens, a jumble of old bills which she flicks through half-heartedly, gas, electricity, phone, empty matchboxes, kipple. When she puts them all back, she notices something under the cloth on the bottom and so lifts it up to investigate. She thinks she's looking into a mirror, but no, it's a photograph. There she is, herself, in Ital Park, hugging Lascano, both of them smiling at the camera. She falls back on the bed; now she's the one who's seen a ghost. She goes into the bathroom and looks back and forth between her reflection in the mirror and the photo. Now she understands why this man protects her, helps her. She realizes that the woman must have left him or died, almost certainly the latter because Lascano has the burnt-out look of a widower before his time, and she can appreciate why he doesn't know what to do with her. Everything becomes clear, and she goes back to his bed to study the photo at greater length. They look happy and in love, while behind them a roller coaster descends at full speed, a blur of fuchsia, green and yellow lights, the people's faces terrified and out of focus. Lascano has a lovely smile she has never seen before. His skin shines in contrast to the mate coloured complexion he has these days and she understands his pain of happiness lost. A salt tear falls on the photo and mixes with the silver salts that preserve the image. She slumps back on the bed, buries herself in the pillow, which smells of him, and she cries and cries for her pain, until night starts to fall. She sleeps and in her dream Lascano, the child growing inside her, the woman in the snapshot and Eva herself all get confused. There is a park where the grass meets the sea, where everything is pleasant, sincere and warm.

Sounds. Eva leaps up, hides the photo and slips out of the bedroom as Lascano, with his back to her, closes the front door. She pretends to come out of the bathroom, her heart punching her from within and her cheeks all flushed. A smile begins to form on his face, but is gone so fast it might have been an illusion. It is as if he suddenly

97

remembered a grave and sad obligation. There then occurs that moment when a man's and a woman's eyes meet and they both realize that things are starting to get serious. Each of them tries to sidestep the revelation and move at the same time, their bodies colliding: desire has dug its teeth in and won't let go, even if for now they both retreat into their own shells. She at least has the child warming her belly. He only has a photo, which he finds under his pillow without wondering how it got there, accustomed as he is to Marisa sneaking up on him any time, any place. In the lounge, Eva wants to laugh and she wants to cry, while falling asleep on the sofa. *Tomorrow's another day,* as her granny, happy to state the obvious, would always say when she came to comfort Eva with a goodnight kiss.

13

She didn't hear him leave. When she opens the venetian blinds, a beautiful Thursday pours into the room and makes her feel full of life. The clock tells her she's been asleep for twelve hours straight. Her body is grateful. She thinks of Lascano, his sadness, his not knowing how to handle her, what to do with this replica of his lover, who has appeared before him, who he looks after as if somehow protecting his dead wife. The guy's old enough to be her father. But he's not her father and Eva's always been attracted to older men. In secondary school, when her friends were busy whispering about the boys in the fifth form, she was fantasizing about the other girls' fathers. She found smile lines at the corner of a man's eyes more seductive than the affected posturing of an adolescent, always trying to leave boyhood behind, always trying to appear manlier than he was. Eva was more drawn to the mature man, well-groomed, whose inner child expressed itself freely and willingly rather than betrayed him when least expected.

Wrapped in a flowery headscarf that puts ten years on her, and pulling a shopping trolley, Eva leaves the flat. She goes to a market which every Thursday shuts a nearby street off from the roaring traffic. Free market imports overflow at the colourful fruit stalls: mangoes, plums, pears, papayas and melons, all readily available in the depths of winter. Greengrocers stand on their little platforms shouting out offers, butchers flatter the women with compliments, distracting them while they fiddle the scales. It's all a world apart, a half-day reprieve from the mad city, an oasis of mandarin oranges that lets the little servant girls stock up on fruit and veg. *Look what lovely eggs*, an impish country voice calls out as Eva passes by. And the eggs really do look lovely. Big, brown, smooth. *Come on, madam, take some home with you, they're double yokes.*

She spends the afternoon in the kitchen. Working from memory, something her grandma once showed her, Eva puts an eye round of beef in the oven, stuffed with bacon, garlic, parsley and carrots, surrounded by potatoes. Ten minutes in the oven on a high heat until golden, then an hour at medium temperature and it's ready to eat. Something simple and tasty as a treat for her protector. Why? Because he looks after her, and because he'll be her safe conduct out of the nightmare the country has become, about which she wishes to think no more, and also just because. She wants to head far away and imagines herself on a beach with her daughter enjoying the sunset, loving her little girl and somehow being able to explain to her that she'll not have to go through what her mother went through. *And what if it's a boy?* Things become complicated because Eva can't picture herself with a boy. *How do you talk to a little man? About what?* And so for the purpose of her dreams she decides it'll be a girl, *and if it turns out to be a boy then so be it.*

The house fills up with the smell of cooking. Eva feels like it's a Sunday and she realizes she's longing for

Lascano to arrive home, that actually he's usually home by now. The feeling that something has happened prods her in the chest, but at that very moment he opens the door.

Don't look. I've got a surprise for you. What is it? If I tell you what it is, it won't be a surprise. Close your eyes and give me your hand. Come on, girl, stop with your silliness. I'm not being silly, I've been busy all afternoon. Well, let's see. You can open them now. Well, what have we here? I made it all by myself. OK, wow, let's try it out then.

With the precision of a surgeon, Perro carves through the roast beef, which steams on the plate, lying on its bed of vegetables. He cuts himself the perfect slice that includes part of the vegetables, red meat from the middle and a fine crispy crust, and pops it in his mouth. *The girl certainly chose a good cut. Oh, glorious Argentinean beef! The perfect consistency; not as tender and yielding as sirloin so you have to work it a little, crush it with your molars so that it releases its juices onto your tongue, with the subtle fragrance of garlic and parsley.* The hearty fare slips down his throat and comforts his soul. At meal times he reverts to being a little boy home from school. Lascano pours some wine. Eva patiently awaits his verdict.

Aren't you having some? It's turned out perfect. You like it? It's delicious.

Lascano's gaze wanders from the meat to the spuds to the glass to Eva's eyes, to her mouth and he smiles sincerely.

Honestly, you've excelled. You clearly know how to handle a piece of meat.

His insinuation slips out without warning.

Speaking of meat, the best part's still to come. Oh yes, what's that then? Dessert. Did you make dessert too? The idea is we make it together. With what ingredients? Mystery, silence, the wind and the rain. And does this dessert have a name? It's French, it's called petite mort. *I didn't know you spoke French. There are lots of things you don't know about me. That's true. Well, aren't you curious? A little... When are you going to realize I'm dying for you to make a move on me? Girl, I prefer you being alive. Are you going to play the fool for much longer? For as long as I can. And why, might I ask? Forgive me, but I'm not suited to all these things any more. All what things? These romantic things, dinner, looks, insinuations. Everyone's suited to these things. Those who aren't, are dead already, just nobody told them. You're probably right. You're scared. I know how the story ends. Oh really. So tell me, if you already know, how does it end? With one or both of us suffering. And so? Maybe you like suffering, I don't. Well, if that's your attitude, why don't you just kill yourself? What's that got to do with anything? You're going to die one day, you know. We're all going to die one day. Not loving for fear of suffering is like not living for fear of dying. The young lady is a philosopher? Sir is a coward? Don't be like that. And how else do you expect me to be? Do you think I don't notice the way you look at me? You silly old fool, you've got desire written all over your face. You said the word: old. I'm too old for you. It's true I like you, you're really very lovely, but I'm not fit for that sort of thing any more. But this is ridiculous. I've killed myself preparing you a nice surprise, done nothing but make insinuations and advances and you won't react to a single one of them. What's the matter, do I disgust you? Of course not, how could you possibly disgust me? It's just that love is a very dangerous thing. But stop and look at yourself for a second. A guy who spends all day dealing with criminals and killers is scared of a few caresses. Well this really is a surprise. Armed confrontations, one-on-one shoot-outs, they leave me as cold as a fish, but I do take aversion to mass killings, to catastrophes. And what, love is a catastrophe? Forgive me, but yes, it's a catastrophe. Don't you realize that it's the only thing you've got? Don't give me that stupid look. We're alive, right now, alone, you like me, I like you. You've got the hots for me, I've got the hots for you. That's all that exists. Tomorrow we could both be dead. What are you waiting for, a hearse? I'm not waiting for anything. Well, go cry on your own then, die on your own. You're really pissed off with me? Yes, very. Is this a fight? No, it's a comic strip. This is just the first of many. The second. Well, I must admit, I'd spend my whole life fighting with you. You see? We've already gone mad. And who wants to be sane at a time like this?*

Silence. Lascano, tucked into one corner of the sofa, pretends to be fascinated by the end of his shoes. In the other corner, straddled over the arm, Eva stares at him. Every one of her muscles is tense. She takes a breath and relaxes, then lets herself fall softly into the chair, kicking him as she does so. She's not going to let him get away that easily. He raises his head, his misty eyes fill her with a mixture of pity and anger. What she needs right now is a man. She moves closer, he says: *stop this nonsense*. She, *OK*, and she puts her arms around his neck and closes in on his face and they press their lips together and while her smells rush to his head – horny bitch, whore, mother, sister, daughter – her breasts nestle into his torso and he opens his mouth so that she can stick her tongue inside, his body softens after so many longed-for caresses, so many nights alone, and he feels touched by hands that are not his own, hands full of surprises – *where are they going now?* – with new rhythms, with snatched breaths and his sex is triumphantly reborn and wants to fly and it grows painful wings, it grabs hold of her and she responds reciting…

...and then I asked him with my eyes to ask again yes
and then he asked me would I yes to say yes my mountain
flower
and first I put my arms around him yes
and drew him down to me so he could feel my breasts all
perfume yes
and his heart was going like mad
and yes I said yes I will Yes.

...and he feels like a man once more, now is the moment, and they are already naked and their skins touch rub bristle and their half-open mouths breathe steam and the lights get brighter until finally they have to break their embrace to dim the lights because in the semi-darkness you see better and this brief separation brings back memories of many other separations and begs their salty bodies to be reunited and pleads for one to quickly become embedded with the other and the loaded flesh to enter the loved flesh bringing about a grimace of the sweetest pain and a vampire stare and who is who now? my little he-man inhabited female thighs like pincers rigid muscles everything a melody of veins and bones and hair and running blood and I want more and more and give me everything my whore and he kisses her lips and puts his fingers in their mouths so that his hands can attest to this game of tongues fluids that come and go and grow and multiply and from below there emerge smells of the sea of molluscs of sudden storms and the sand after the rain and they want to lose themselves one in the other go deeper to recover paradise lost and they say kill me or you are killing me and I feel death and hug me tight don't leave me here you're real there is no reality other than this pleasure and this pain and they are the rain and the earth, the earth which will finally devour us all but for now the earth is soaked in song and they are the beast with two backs in need of caresses as they are at the mercy of the elements riding the home stretch where faintness and total confusion of the senses are one and the same when I smell I touch I feel I sense and completion and slowly the embrace slackens to allow respective souls to return to respective bodies leaving love scars and traces of solitude on the other. Never say I love you.

Lascano, there's something I have to tell you.

Go on.

I'm pregnant.

So soon?

14

Amancio parks his estate on the side street. The cold anger he has felt since arguing with Lara is reflected in the cool of the night. He walks slowly and angrily to the corner. The glare of emergency lights hits him like an electric shock. On the opposite pavement, two green Ford Falcons are double parked, their portable flashing lights on their roofs. Amancio steps back a couple of paces, into the shade of the plantain trees. Next to one of the cars is a young man, dressed in civilian clothes, Ithaca shotgun in hand. Further on, in front of a block of flats, another carries a PAM.

He feels a shiver go down his spine. He's reminded of how unstable and jumpy those machine guns are, the time he had a go with one at the army shooting range with Giribaldi. Shots fired out suddenly without him having moved, never mind touched the trigger. The PAM just started spitting bullets out of its own accord. It was only by the grace of God that Amancio didn't end up shooting himself or anyone else present. Since the incident, he had always viewed these weapons with a mixture of respect and suspicion. He would also never forget the sound of Giribaldi's military friends, laughing their heads off at the fright he'd given himself.

Four armed men leave the building, a frightened couple in tow. He gropes the air like a blind man. She's shoved into the back seat of the second car. They let him loose in front of the first car. A man who seems to be in charge of the operation barks an order at him: *Get in.* The guy probes the air nervously with his hands, then one of his captors pushes him so that he bangs into the car door. They all laugh. Amancio is surprised to learn there are blind subversives, *but, well, you never do know.* Eventually, they stuff the blind man into the back of the car and force him to the floor. The armed men jump in and the two Falcons drive off. Before the cars reach the next corner, the lights have been taken off the roofs.

Amancio walks up to the Bitermans' block and opens the door with the key that Horacio gave him. A smell of food fills the landing. Something fried that Amancio finds disgusting. The rhythmic sound made by the lift as it climbs, *bum bum,* seems to keep time with Amancio's heartbeat, which is getting faster and faster. He can feel every systolic beat pounding in his neck and brow. His vision is blurred, a combination of the alcohol he drank to give him courage and the fury that lingers from his row with Lara and her departure. He knows he's not in the best state to do what he's planning to do, that he's a little unsteady. He breathes quickly and loudly to get some air in his lungs.

As he gets out on the fourth floor, he doesn't notice that he's being spied on by the neighbour through the peephole. The shutter closes as soon as he goes into Biterman's office.

The moneylender is sitting at the desk revising his accounts, when he suddenly becomes aware of Amancio's presence, gun in hand. Not looking the least unsettled, he peers at him from above his reading glasses.

What are you doing here, how did you get in? That doesn't matter. I've come to cancel my debts. Hand over the cheques. OK. Stay calm. I've got them here. Don't try anything clever. Put your right hand on your left shoulder then slowly open the drawer with your left hand. You want the cheques and I'm going to give them to you. Come on then, let's have them.

Without taking his eyes off Amancio for a second, Biterman gradually opens the drawer. Amancio feels like his face is on fire. He can't see what's in the drawer. He moves up on to his tiptoes to try to make sure the Jew doesn't have a gun in there. Biterman realizes that in doing so, Amancio is no longer pointing the gun at him and he decides to take advantage of the situation. The beast breaks loose and lets forth a savage roar that has Amancio rooted to the spot. With a fierce swipe, Biterman sends the nine millimetre crashing out of Amancio's hand. He heaves the desk over, sending papers flying in a rain of giant confetti, and throws himself on top of Amancio with all his strength and weight, knocking him to the floor. Amancio tries to resist, but he lands with his legs all twisted underneath him and Biterman disables him further by yanking his arm behind his back like a lever. Biterman's enormous buffalo head spits with fury, inches from Amancio's face. Amancio tries to wriggle free with desperate movements that do nothing but provoke a slight smile from Biterman. Amancio feels like a crushed ant. His legs start to cramp.

Did you really think that you, you toffee-nosed prick, could frighten me with a gun? I'm going to ram it up your arse, then you'll learn. All right. All right? You pathetic fool. Hooray Henry. You can thank your lucky stars I'm a businessman. If I kill you, I won't get paid.

Suddenly Biterman pummels Amancio's ears hard with both fists, stunning him. Biterman grabs the gun, jumps up and kicks him in the ribs. Amancio gasps like a fish out of water

And I have to tell you that this little incident has not only doubled your debt, but made the deadline expire. So here's what we're going to do. Tomorrow, nice and early, you're going to call the notary and take him the deeds to La Rencorosa. From now on, it's mine. But Biterman... Mr Biterman to you. Come on, stop fucking around. Does it look like I'm fucking around to you? No. Good. You'd better be damned sure I'm not.

Biterman looks at Amancio as if contemplating an insect and allows him to get his breath back. Amidst much coughing, Amancio finally manages to raise himself off the floor and sit up straight. From where Biterman is standing, he can kick or punch Amancio at will, should he try anything. Amancio is completely flustered by the transformation he has brought about in the Jew. Biterman has the glowing eyes of a wild animal and his mouth is somehow contorted into a strange smile, which emphasizes very white teeth and two sharp canines. Although Biterman now speaks and acts with his usual serenity, his muscles remain taut and imply violence. Completely intimidated, Amancio nervously watches Biterman's giant feet and hands while rubbing his own cracked ribs. When Biterman bends down to pick something up off the floor, Amancio's whole being flinches. Biterman cuts the emphatic figure of a boxer towering over his floored opponent, knocked-out, no way back.

No need to be so jumpy, I just wanted to pass you these papers to sign. Make yourself comfortable and add your signature, at the side of this page and at the bottom of this one. But they're

blank? What if I refuse? You leave here feet first. Where am I signing? There and there... good. Give me them... Happy now? Can I go? One more thing. How did you get in? ... Come on idiot. Can't you see I've got your life in my hands? Answer. How did you get in? Horacio. The other little maggot. I thought as much.

Biterman grabs Amancio by the lapels and pulls him to his feet. A shove sends Amancio crashing into the wall, producing a deep wound on the temple, which gushes blood into his eye. Biterman spins him around like a doll and throws him out of the room. Amancio, utterly dazed, departs with comical dance steps. Another push sends him flying towards the door, making him slump to the floor. Biterman pulls the door open hard, striking Amancio once again. He then grabs Amancio by the seat of his trousers and hurls him out, face first, into the corridor wall, plaster crumbling down and sticking to the blood on his forehead. Standing tall and dominant, Biterman takes the magazine from the gun and puts it in his pocket. He then carefully wipes the pistol down with a handkerchief. His experience has taught him to loathe guns, and his wisdom to stay clear of them. When he finishes rubbing off all traces of himself, he slings the weapon at Amancio's head. Amancio anticipates this and blocks the throw with his hands. The nine millimetre bounces down between his legs.

Have it back little boy, go and play Cowboys and Indians.

The slam of the door echoes down the corridor. Amancio feels the pain of every blow as he struggles to his feet. Fear starts to change to fury. He thinks of everything that will happen next. He has lost La Rencorosa and in a few days time, when his other creditors find out, and they will find out, the floodgates will open and lawsuits will pour down upon him. He pictures Lara, waving goodbye as he's carted off in handcuffs. He takes a step; the after-effect of the twisted leg brings an acute flash of pain. He leans against the wall, plaster dusting his tattered blue jacket with a layer of grey. He feels like crying and screaming. He looks for a tissue in his pocket to stem the flow of blood from his face. His hand comes across the leftover bullet. He picks up the gun and slots the cartridge straight into the chamber. Then he takes off his jacket and wraps it around the gun. He moves forward a step, and gives two hard knocks on the door. He hears footsteps approaching. He steps back, supports himself against the wall and holds the gun up in front of him, draped in the coat. The door swings open, the Jew's imposing figure filling its frame. Amancio closes his eyes tight and pulls the trigger. Biterman stares at his stomach in disbelief. Then he looks up, leaps forward and grabs Amancio by the neck. Amancio feels Biterman's hands turn to pliers as they cut off his air supply. He punches Biterman in the sides but the pressure on his throat doesn't let up. His strength starts to desert him and he feels a sense of resignation. Suddenly, Biterman's eyes open extremely wide and a line of blood trickles out of his half-open mouth. A stupefied look transforms his face, his hands relax, his head drops forward onto Amancio's chest and his breath starts to choke. He lets out a deep, harsh sound, his muscles slacken, his body makes a few spasmodic kicks and then he falls, dragging Amancio down with him. Smothered by Biterman's inert body, Amancio tries to get his breath back. He fights himself free from the dead man and staggers to his feet. The lights suddenly come on in the hallway and, as he pants heavily, Amancio hears the lift heading for the ground floor. He grabs hold of Biterman by the legs, drags him inside the apartment, closes the door and slumps into a chair. There he remains for he doesn't know how long, staring at the body, trying to recover, sharp pains attacking him all over.

When he's feeling a bit more composed, he gets up and goes into the bathroom. His face is covered in cuts and bruises. The moneylender's fingers have marked his neck. He turns on the tap and splashes his face over and over again. With a towel, he cleans the blood that continues to flow from his eyebrow. He puts pressure on the wound and then goes back into the other room to reassure himself that Biterman is definitely dead. He sits down again. He thinks, thinks *what do I do now?* A solution occurs to him. He goes back into the bathroom and tidies himself up as best he can. He leaves the flat.

The cold night air allows him to regain a degree of self-control, what little he has left. He's shaking all over. He quickly breathes in and out several times. He walks a short distance, then sits down on the steps of the next building to allow himself time to recuperate.

A white Mercedes 1518 is parked across the street, outside the building where the blind man and the woman were brought out. Two pieces of brown paper, torn apart by someone's teeth, are pasted on its doors, crudely covering the navy insignia. Various conscripts come in and out carrying furniture, a fridge, a television, cases, a range of domestic appliances, and they put everything in the back of the truck, supervised by an arrogant blond captain. Amancio starts to feel more like himself, gets to his feet, crosses the road, enters a café and goes over to the pay phone. The Spanish owner, mechanically wiping the bar with a dish cloth, calls over to him.

Don't waste your time. I asked them to fix it three months ago and I'm still waiting. You can use this one here if you leave some coins for the call. Thanks a lot.

The barman places the telephone on the bar and thinks *this guy has obviously just taken a beating*. But as it's got nothing to do with him, in a deliberate show of discretion, he goes over to rub down the tables, as if they really needed doing.

Hi, Giri... Amancio... Nothing... Very bad... The Yid wasn't such a chicken... I had to... Yes... What shall I do?... Fucking hell, I need your help... Can you drop by here?... In a bar, on the corner where Irigoyen meets Pichincha... Yeah, near the square... Get going. I'll wait for you... OK.

Amancio finds a table by the window from where he can keep an eye on Biterman's block and the coming and going of the conscripts loading the lorry. Now they're carrying pictures, rugs, pots and pans. He orders a Bols, which the Spaniard serves up to the brim of a small sturdy glass. Amancio downs it in one and orders another. The nasty spirit warms his gullet and gradually he stops shaking. The pains become more localized, less general, and a splitting headache sets upon him, which he thinks he might dull with a third gin. Other than the marine removal men, the street is empty. With some satisfaction, he thinks about how Biterman's body will have already begun to decompose, filling up with worms until he disappears. Making him disappear, this is the problem Amancio now faces. He could just leave him there and let Horacio deal with the mess in the morning, after all... But he doesn't trust him. As soon as the police put any pressure on, Horacio would no doubt tell them everything, act the innocent and dump the whole load on Amancio. On the other hand, if there is no corpse, there's no proof of the crime and no conviction, even if a trail does lead to Amancio. Yes, the Jew has to disappear. And now that he's dead, Amancio has solved the problem of the cheques. Come to think of it, he has to go back and get the cheques, and the blank pieces of paper he was made to sign. He feels about in his pockets in sudden panic and sighs in relief that he still has the keys. Giribaldi knows what to do with dead bodies.

Meanwhile, now on his fourth gin, a warm drowsiness comes over him. Gretschen pops into his head, a girl who already had a prize pair of tits at the age of fourteen. Horse rides on their uncle and auntie's ranch out at Tapalqué. His cousin galloping along the cattle tracks, her boobs bouncing up and down in front of his twelve-year-old eyes. Lying in the clover, she would let him touch them and kiss her with closed lips and say they were a secret couple, because if cousins have children then they turn out defective, so no one must know. At night around the dining table, the day's sun still warm on their skin, they would exchange naughty looks and, later on, once the sheets warmed up, Amancio would take hold of his sex with thumb and forefinger and masturbate slowly imagining that Gretschen, in the next room, was doing the same thinking of him. And then, with veritable joy, he would release the millions of children they would never have into the piece of toilet paper he'd brought in from the bathroom.

He gives a sudden start. Giri, in military fatigues, is knocking on the window. Amancio signals for him to come in. The military man sits down in front of him, orders a hot chocolate and looks out at the navy lorry.

Looks like someone's moving house. Looks that way.

Giribaldi notices the injuries on Amancio's face.

What happened? When he saw the weapon he went mental and jumped on top of me. These Jews, they get cheekier by the day. You don't say. What shall I do? Look, right now I can't help you because I've got a job on myself. And so? Let me think. Are you in your car? It's around the corner. Good. Load up the stiff and take it for a drive for a while. You know the road that goes alongside the Riachuelo? The one we used to take to the racetrack? Exactly. Right, we'll be transferring some extremists there later on. You'll find a little corrugated iron hut, half falling down. Next to it is a dirt track. Head down it, into the scrubland. You'll see some leftists who've been dumped there. Leave your Jew with them. And then what? Go home. I'll take care of making them all disappear. You can't imagine how grateful I am. What are friends for? Look, I've got to go. Be careful, don't let anybody see you. This lot seems to be finishing up. As soon as they're gone, load up the Yid and take him for a spin. Then at around seven dump him where I said. Consider it done. And be careful, yeah? Don't worry about it. Make sure you do worry about it though. You owe me one. I sure do. Bye then, old buddy. He really made you mad, the Yid, then? Lend me something to pay for this would you? I have to lend you cash as well? C'mon, give me a break. Here you go, now you owe me two.

All dapper in his immaculate uniform, Giribaldi jumps in his car and ploughs away. The soldiers finish loading the truck. Amancio asks for the bill, pays and leaves. A gust of wind whips at him as he crosses the road and he shivers as he enters the building where Biterman lies dead.

Amancio's a little repulsed by the idea that he'll have to touch a dead body. He tugs the curtain down and laboriously wraps the corpse in it, then uses the curtain ties to fasten up the package. He sits down. The fabric starts to stain with blood. He gets up. He goes out into the corridor. He presses the button on the Otis elevator. When the lift arrives, Amancio opens the door. He goes back. With great effort, he drags the body to the lift and then, also with much difficulty, manages to get it inside. He closes the door and starts the descent. He thinks he sees Biterman move. He thinks he hears a whine. Terrified, he starts kicking the bundle where he supposes the head is. He reaches the ground floor. He gets out of the lift. He closes the interior grill. With one hand he holds down the latch to make the lift think the door is closed. He puts his other hand through the bars of the grill and presses a button in the lift. He pulls his hand back quickly and watches the lift go up, then lets go of the door latch with the other hand. The lift halts between two floors. With the butt of his gun he shifts the lever that blocks the door when the lift is on another floor, and doesn't realise he's damaged the breech. He closes the lift door and goes out into the street.

Amancio realizes he's started shaking again and he tells himself it's because of the physical effort of moving the carcass. He walks to the corner. Turns. Gets in his car, puts it into reverse, his foot slips off the clutch, the car jumps back and bashes into the truck parked behind. He gets out. He's put a dent in his rear door and broken one of the brake lights. He gets back behind the wheel, pulls off, drives around the block and parks. He gets out. Goes in.

He pulls open the lift door. With one hand he holds down the door latch and with the other he presses the button to call the lift. The lift descends. It arrives. He opens the grill. He hears a noise in the street. He climbs into the lift. He closes the door and holds the handle tight so that it can't be opened. The sound of footsteps. Somebody, a resident, tries to open the door, bangs on it. Finally the stranger heads for the staircase, grumbling. Amancio pokes his head out, listens until the sound of footsteps fades away. He heads over to the entrance and jams the door open with a clothes peg. He goes out onto the pavement; the neighbourhood is deserted. He opens the boot of his Rural. He carries the corpse out and puts it in the back, the effort of which produces a sharp pain in his chest, a moment of panic as he feels like his heart is going to explode. He takes the tarpaulin he uses to cover the car in the country in winter and drapes it over the bundle. He goes back to the building, removes the peg, the door swings shut with a thump. He gets into the car, starts up and pulls away.

Amancio's heartbeat thunders in his ears. He's sweating, he sees himself wild-eyed in the mirror. He winds the window down. The winter air hits him full in the face. He hits a pothole that squeezes the shock absorbers to the limit. The steering wheel conveys the city's neglect. He pulls out onto Entre Ríos, driving slowly down the middle of the street. He inhales deeply, counts to ten, lets the air out, does it again, and again. *The cheques, the cheques. Bloody hell, I forgot the cheques!*

It's starting to get light. The time has come. He gets to Vélez Sarsfield, drives around the bridge and he's beside the stagnant river. He takes a perfumed tissue out of his pocket and drives with one hand on the wheel, the other holding the tissue over his nose to cover up the putrid smell. He remembers that his father used to make the same joke whenever they passed the Riachuelo: *Breathe in boys, it's good for a cough.* It's a grey morning and he can't see more than twenty feet in front of the car, the fog acting like a wall refracting the car's headlights. He turns them off, reduces his speed. *How the hell am I going to find the hut in this kind of visibility.* And then he sees it. It's like a brown brushstroke on a canvas of grey. He brakes. He reverses back up the road until he passes the hut again, then noses forward down the dirt track towards it. Before he's gone far, he spots the bulk of something. Two corpses lie on the ground. Competing winds start to sweep away the fog. The girl's head has been destroyed with gunshots and part of her brain has spilled out onto what remains of her face. He feels himself retch and turns away. He doesn't want to see any more. He opens the boot and faces up to the gruelling task of getting Biterman out. He takes the tarpaulin off. The movement of the car has made the curtain slide off the dead body, leaving the Jew's blood-soaked belly on full display. As he pulls at the corpse, he finds one of its arms has got jammed under the spare tyre. To Amancio, it seems like the dead man is refusing to let go. He wrestles with it, but only succeeds in getting the arm stuck even more. He looks for the key that unfastens the screw that holds the tyre in place. He finally manages to free the arm and pull the body halfway out of the car. He grabs hold of the dead man's belt and pulls. The buckle snaps. Amancio throws the strip of leather away in anger. He grabs hold of Biterman by the legs and drags him out of the car. He unties and unwraps the body, not wanting to leave the curtain behind, and he notices that the corpse is already starting to go stiff. He gets his breath back. He rolls the fabric into a ball and hurls it into the river. The water begins to stain it, then

119

swallows it up. Slowly the bundle sinks, becomes a ghost and disappears.

Amancio gets into the car and reverses up the track. As he reaches the street, he notices a car approaching with its lights on. He takes the same lane and pulls away at top speed. In the rear-view mirror, the lights of the other car quickly get smaller and smaller until they can no longer be seen. He slows down and carries on towards General Paz. All he can think of is a whisky, a bath and bed.

15

Lascano arrives at police headquarters when everyone else is getting ready to go home. He wants to go through certain dossiers when the archives department is at its quietest, so that he can work unobserved and avoid having to check files in and out at the desk, preferring to leave no record of his research. Office work, what he likes least.

Five hours of reading have blurred his vision and five hours of chain smoking have filled his lungs with soot. He sets off walking from headquarters to his car, parked on the end block of Diagonal Norte. He's nearly there when he gets mixed up with the audience coming out of the late showing at Cine Arte. He notices *Pasqualino Setebelleze* on the billing and starts to weave his way through the crowd when a scream draws everyone's attention.

Across the road, a man holding a shotgun is standing beside a double-parked Ford Falcon. Two other men come out of an apartment block with their pistols drawn, dragging along a young man who cries out again and manages to pull himself free. One of the armed men swings a punch but misses. The youth runs out into the middle of the street, but when he's halfway between the cinema-goers and his pursuers he trips, falls and is recaptured. He shouts out his name. One of the men lunges at the boy and hits him on the head with his gun. The men with pistols carry him over to the Falcon and throw him in the back. The man with the shotgun points it at the crowd and growls something that can't be understood but that everyone understands and the group starts to disperse. Lascano, alone on the pavement, watches the Falcon turn onto Libertad and quickly disappear.

Where Diagonal ends, behind the leafy eucalyptuses on Plaza Lavalle, the solemn Palace of Justice stands tall, blind, dirty and deaf.

16

Lascano likes the suburbs. They're the essence of his youth. Nobody knows these places and these people better than he does. Out here people still have a provincial air, but it's spiked with the cynicism that emanates from the big city, just twenty minutes up the Panamerican highway. Ponds, stray dogs, a bar where men sit playing hands of *Tutte Cabrero*, Guigue the pools coupon man on the street corner, the bottle collector pulling his cart.

But it's not nostalgia that has brought Lascano here. A cast-iron arch adorns the entrance and above it a sheet-metal sign announces the Fortuna Sawmill, in rather pretentious shaded lettering. This is the only clue offered by the corpse planted at the scene of the execution. As if in a scene from a film noir, Perro takes out the business card and looks up at the sign. Here is where he hopes to find the end of the thread that will unravel the crime. This is the place all right.

Dodging the potholes full of water and rotting wood shavings spilled by the freight lorries, he moves forward purposefully. He is guided by the screech of an electric saw as it cuts through a board, held by a huge blond man in overalls. The man's missing the top of his index finger on his right hand and a cataract in one of his eyes has turned the pupil white. The guy is so concentrated on the saw edge he seems not to notice Lascano's presence. But without stopping his work he suddenly speaks.

And how may I be of service, Superintendent? Good morning.

Lascano takes out the photo of Biterman and throws it onto the bench.

Do you know this man?

The woodcutter closes his cloudy eye and half-heartedly glances at the photo with the other.

Biterman. Pardon? Biterman, a moneylender. Do you know him? Is he dead? As dead as Gardel. What's your relationship with him? When I was flat broke he cashed me cheques. So someone finally went and killed him. How do you know someone killed him? If he'd died of the flu I doubt you'd be here. Do you know anyone who might have had a motive to kill him? Yes. Who? Me... and half the phone book. The guy was a swine. Honestly, I'm glad he's pushing up daisies. Did you kill him? Just my luck, someone got there before me. Where were you Tuesday night? You see the bar across the way? Go in there and ask. I was watching the beating Galíndez gave Skog. As well as the owners and the waiter, there were at least twenty others in there. We stayed pretty late. Did they televize it? Now that you come to mention it, no, we actually listened to the fight on the radio. It's just that the commentator... Cafaretti. That's the one, Cafaretti, he describes it so well you feel like you're ringside. Do you have the address of this... Biterman? Sure do. Gladys! What? Give this man the Yid's address. Thanks a lot.

Lascano heads towards the girl hidden away in the "office". The voice of the carpenter booms out over his shoulder.

If you do catch whoever killed Biterman, tell him I'll pay for his lawyer.

17

And what's all the mystery in aid of? It's a surprise. Another one? This one's different. Come on. Where are we going? To the place where you found me. The brothel? Exactly. Are you going to tell me what this is all about? Not until we get there. Shrouded in secrecy. You have to make a promise.

She looks lovely and he's ready to promise her anything.

I'm going to show you something I found when I was hiding and you were busting the brothel. OK. What I found is very important. What is it? Let me finish. You haven't said your vows yet. Go on. I want you to promise that we'll keep what I show you for us, just for you and me. But what is it? Promise. All right, I promise. Good, let's go then.

The street is empty. They quickly get out of the car, cross the road and pull down the crime-scene tape stuck across the green door to Tony Ventura's bordello.

We are committing a crime, Eva. The crime was meeting you in the first place.

Lascano follows her up the stairs to the room with the false socket.

Close your eyes. Again? Close them. OK, they're closed. Surprise!

Lascano opens his eyes, Eva's hand waves the two wads of dollar bills.

Holy shit! And what's this? Money to buy bird food. It must be a very hungry bird. It's starving. Girl, we have to hand this in. You promised. And anyway, hand it in to who? I don't know... to the law. What law? Don't look at me like that, it's not ours. It is, it says so here, pay the bearer. It belongs to whoever is holding it. I don't know. I do, you look after it, but remember it's both of ours. OK, but we'll decide what we're going to do with it later. Secure our future is what we're going to do with it. We'll have to think about that. You think about it all you want. I'll make you see sense. For now, I have to go and see your friend, the one who's going to help me with the documents. Do you want me to give you a lift? Please.

18

Lascano crosses the road, squeezes his cigarette butt between thumb and forefinger and tosses it into the little stream running in the gutter. The doorman is a tight-lipped country boy who immediately recognizes Lascano as a policeman. Lascano's just as quick to work out the porter is an ex-con, but he decides not to question him for now. Perro walks past and they pointedly ignore each other, monitoring one another all the while. The building is silent. Lascano gets in the lift. The grill jams when he tries to draw it shut. There's a small triangular chink of something stuck in the groove, stopping it from sliding smoothly. He bends down to pick up the offending item. It's a little piece of perforated plastic with the quarter part of a hole, evidently the fixing for a screw. He's pretty sure it belongs to the handle of a gun. He puts it in his pocket. He tries the grill again and, much to his satisfaction, it slides shut with ease.

Good morning, I'm Superintendent Lascano. Good morning, Superintendent, how can I help you? Is this Mr Biterman's address? Mr Biterman at your service. You're Biterman? I am. I'm looking for a different Biterman. That'll be my brother. Is he around? He hasn't arrived yet. Can I come in? Be my guest. When did you last see your brother? Tuesday afternoon.

While Horacio turns to shut the door, Lascano takes the Polaroid out of his pocket and holds it up, ready to observe Horacio's reaction.

Is this your brother? What's happened? He was murdered. But... how...why...who? I was hoping you might be able to answer some of those questions. I don't know who could have done such a thing. He was a much loved guy, never upset anyone. What kind of a business is this? Finance. So I see. Things going well for you? Modestly, we can't complain. Were you and your brother partners? I'm an employee. Do you mind if I have a quick look around? Is it really necessary? I can come back with a search warrant and ten other officers if you'd prefer. No, there's no need for that, go right ahead.

Keeping his hands in his pockets to be sure not to touch anything, Lascano explores the office, which seems to be a bit too tidy. Something tells him it's not normally like this. On top of the desk is a chequebook for the Banco de Crédito Comercial. He notices that the corner of the desk is splintered and that the damage seems recent because the laceration sprouts hairs of fresh wood. On the wall there's a black stain that someone has tried to clean up. Lascano would like to confirm it's still damp but Horacio's watching him like a hawk so he resists the temptation. He walks past Horacio in silence. The curtain rail has fallen down and a shred of cloth hangs from it.

Did he have family? Just me. Enemies? None I knew of. Well, I don't want to trouble you any more at this painful time. But I will need to talk to you again. Whenever you like. Would you be able to come down to the mortuary to identify the body? When would you like me there? Tomorrow at eleven suit you? Fine. Do you know where it is? No. Viamonte, 2151. I'll find it. Was your brother rich? Let's say he was fairly well off. And how about you? I get by. See you tomorrow at eleven then.

By the time he leaves, Lascano's convinced Elías was killed in the Bitermans' office. There's no sign of Horacio having been in a struggle, and in any case he seems too faint-hearted for murder, but Lascano has no doubt the brother was instigator, brains or accomplice. As ever, the question is: *Who benefited from this death? Horacio. But there's someone else involved and I have to find out who before putting the pressure on little brother.* These are Lascano's thoughts as he waits for the lift, when he hears a noise to his side. He pretends to cough and with a quick glimpse catches the neighbour's eyes at the little window of the peephole. When he starts to walk over, the shutter closes with a bang. He can see the shadow of feet at the bottom of the door as he knocks lightly with his knuckles. He smiles. The door opens immediately, revealing a woman around seventy years old, tiny but strong and tense. Her hard hands hold a brand new dishcloth. She smells of bleach, is wearing a pinafore and has slippers on her feet. She looks like she's stepped straight out of a detergent commercial.

Good day to you, madam. I'm Superintendent Lascano. What did you say? That I'm Superintendent Lascano, from the police. Oh, sorry, I'm a little deaf, the health service still hasn't got around to authorizing my hearing aid. I need one in order to hear properly these days... Can I come in and talk to you for a minute? And how do I know you're really from the police?

Lascano flashes his badge.

Satisfied? Please come in.

It's a space much like the Bitermans'. The whole flat speaks of an owner obsessed with cleaning. Everything gleams. Through the door opening to the bedroom

Lascano sees the television covered with a plastic sheet. It has a glass cockerel on top that predicts the weather by changing colour. The floor shines. It's easy to guess that a pristine façade hides a mortally boring life, but in spite of this, or maybe precisely because of it, the place is very soothing.

Sorry to bother you. It's no bother. Please take a seat. Thanks. Do you live alone? Yes. I'm widowed. My son lives in Comodoro Rivadavia. He's an engineer. Great. Do you know your neighbours, the Bitermans? If you mean know them in the sense of knowing them, then no, I don't know them. I come across them on the landing from time to time. The younger one is friendly. The elder one never even says hello. He always seems to be on a different planet. What can you tell me about them? Well, they don't live here. They just have their office here. But if you asked me what they did for a living, I wouldn't have a clue. What is true though, is that quite a lot of people come and go. Sometimes they buzz my door on the intercom by mistake. They get confused. I see. And these visitors, what sort of people are they? Older people, always in a hurry. No one stays for longer than ten or fifteen minutes. Don't ask me what they talk about though, because I don't like to meddle in other people's business. Each to their own, that's what I think. But I do know that the two of them don't get on well. You don't say. I do say. You know what these modern apartments are like. The walls are paper thin. Even if you don't want to, you can't help but hear everything. And I'm half-deaf, so just imagine. What have you heard? Now and again voices are raised. I don't pay much attention, but on more than one occasion I've had to bang on the wall to make them stop shouting. It gets as bad as that? The other night they had a terrible fight. I was already in bed. It sounded to me like it came to blows. In fact, I was quite scared. When was this? ...Let me think... Tuesday night. Are you sure? Yes, because it was the day I went to the dentist. And did you see anything? When I got up, I looked out of the peephole, but things had calmed down by then... I was quite shaken... I had to take a pill to get back to sleep. Excellent. Thanks a lot for your help. Has something serious happened? We don't know. A complaint was made and so we're investigating. It was probably nothing more than a brotherly squabble. Yes, of course. Well, I shan't trouble you any more. It's no trouble. Oh, one other thing. I'd prefer it if you didn't mention our little conversation to anyone for the moment. No problem. If you need anything, I'm at your service. Many thanks. Good day. Good day.

19

Marraco's office is on the sixth floor of the courthouse and is reached via an intricate labyrinth of corridors lined with shelves packed with files. Lascano's convinced that justice almost always gets lost somewhere in this sea of papers that come and go like the tides: deadlines, conclusions, official letters, certificates, notifications, notice orders, pigeon hole memos, public prosecutor permits, counsellor permits, days that go by, files that grow thicker, lawyers that issue more and more writs, documents, evidence, court orders, expert opinions, proceedings and more proceedings, until nobody can remember why the whole thing started in the first place, or nobody is left with the will to read through three or four hundred pages. Criminals with the means to hire a skilled lawyer end up going free. The ones who lack the resources end up counting the days to their release dates, learning the error of their ways doing time at "the school", as inmates call Devoto prison, because you learn a lot there.

The judge is showing an office junior how to log the writs in a case file, like those on the racks behind them. He's a lad around seventeen years old, a law student working for free in order to get a foot on the judicial ladder. Lively and curious, he quickly gives Lascano the once over. Lascano likes the look of the kid. A bond forms between them right away. Lascano sits down opposite the judge and, while they chat, he admires the precise movements of the youngster, itemizing and amending.

Superintendent, I have to congratulate you. Operation Gaspar Campos was a total success. Even if some walked. Two. Who were they? A colonel and his deputy. Anyway, you haven't come here for a pat on the back. No, I've come about another matter that also corresponds to you. The three John Does. Two John Does.

Marraco asks the office boy to bring him the file. The judge opens it, flicks through a few pages and then points at a line of text with his finger.

It says three here. But one no longer exists. His name's Biterman, Elías Biterman, he was a moneylender. What's the story then? I got a call because a lorry driver had reported two bodies dumped by the Riachuelo. What are we settling on, two or three? I'm getting there. The guy said two. Uh-huh, and then? Well the thing is, when I got there, an hour later, I found three bodies. Maybe he could only see two from where he was or he got confused. It's possible, but it seems highly unlikely. Why? Two of them were youngsters and had their heads blown to bits. Meaning? Meaning armed forces. Why so? Well, on their sorties, every member of the task force has to shoot the victim in the head. Basically so that they're all implicated... Look, you... Anyway, the fact is that right from the beginning this Biterman caught my attention. His head was intact, the other two were much younger and there were big differences in what they were wearing. Furthermore, while the two kids were wet with dew, Biterman was completely dry. All right, a fair few differences... But that's not all. When I arrived on the scene, I saw a car speeding away. At the time I didn't pay it much attention. But afterwards I started to think that maybe they moved Biterman's body in that car to plant him there. A reasonable assumption. What happened next? Same as usual, I took them to the mortuary. You're a policeman with scruples, Lascano. Is that a compliment? An acknowledgment, anyone else in your position would have buried all three and forgotten the matter. But you, no, you started to investigate. What have you found out? Well, first I established an identity. I also gently questioned the brother of the victim, a certain Horacio, and a neighbour of theirs. And? Of one thing I'm certain. Horacio's involved in his brother's death right to the core. Why do you say that? Biterman was rich. Horacio was his employee. Biterman was a miser. Horacio fancies himself as a playboy. They got on very badly and Horacio's his only inheritor. So we have the motive. What about the opportunity? We still haven't established the time of death. But I would bet my life that Horacio has a cast-iron alibi anyway. He gave me the most unconvincing display of being a grief-stricken brother. So what are you saying? I don't think he killed him, he's too dainty for that, so he must have had at least one accomplice. I'm still working on it, there's a few questions to clear up. Such as? The matter of moving the body and who did it, how did they know that they were going to execute the other two there? It could be pure coincidence. I find it strange, Judge, to hear you of all people speak of coincidences. At one point it occurred to me that maybe the army have been dumping bodies there for a while and the killer knew this. Not a bad theory. But then I rejected the idea. Why? Because I would have heard about it. So you think that Biterman was killed somewhere else and then dumped there to make it look like he was killed by the armed forces. What I think is that someone who was involved in the military operation moved the body, or told Horacio or his accomplice about it. Could well be. But now, Lascano, you, me, everyone, we all know what's going on with subversion. People are being killed all over the place. The guerrillas lay bombs and kill. The army does its thing. You know better than me, that on this matter, we can't do a thing. But with Biterman it's different. I agree, but if there are military personnel mixed up in it, things could get ugly. Biterman's death has nothing to do with subversion or whatever you want to call it. Maybe not. Many people in your position would just forget the whole thing. With so many corpses everywhere, why worry about one more? It's my job. We live in terrible times, it's true. A state of complete confusion, it seems to me. And I must confess that I too get very confused and often don't know what to think for the best. But, you know what? Doing my job focuses me, gives me objectives. If I didn't do it, I think I'd go mad. My only recommendation, Lascano, is that you don't try to act the hero. This thing could get very unpleasant. Do you want me to abandon the investigation? On the contrary, I want you to carry on investigating. But I will ask one thing of you. Fire away. Let's be sensible with it. I'm asking for your discretion. Anything you find out, you tell me first, before you speak to anyone else. We proceed with care. Agreed? You're the boss. I'm amazed at the speed the case is moving forward. I can't decide whether the killers are complete incompetents or whether they think themselves completely above the law, because they've left their grubby paws all over the place. They're probably incompetents who think themselves above the law. Well, you said it. Keep me posted. I should have it solved in a few days.

They depart with a firm handshake. Actually, the firmness comes from Perro, because Marraco's hand is like a jellyfish with manicured nails. Lascano says *see you kid* to the office boy, who responds with a smile that makes Perro feel all fatherly. Marraco, deep in thought, grabs the file.

Hey, kid, go buy me some cigarettes.

He opens a drawer in his desk, puts the file inside and locks it away with a key.

136

20

Have you got the cheques? All right, Amancio, calm down.
A cop's been here. What did he want? They've found Elías.
How? I don't know. What did you do with the body? That's
got nothing to do with you. I put it somewhere safe. Not safe
enough it seems. Damn! I don't understand how this can have
happened. What do we do now? How the hell should I know!
Calm down, idiot, and let me think. You think all you like.
But I have to go to the mortuary and identify the body. And
when I'm there, I'm going to have to deal with this cop. What's
his name? Lezama. Lezama, eh? Right. Don't say a word to
him. Mate, the stiff is my damn brother, I can't just sit there
in silence. And what's more, this guy doesn't miss a trick. He
acts the innocent, but he's a radar, picking up on everything.
Honestly, I think the whole thing has turned very sour. Shut
up, don't be such a chicken. Whose idea was it for me to come
over and threaten your brother anyway? Yours. Who told me he
was terrified of weapons? You. And when I pointed it at him,
he jumped on top of me like an animal. You lied to me, you
son of a bitch, you knew what would happen and you hoped
I'd end up killing him. But Amancio, I swear… Don't bother
swearing anything to me, you're more false than a three-dollar
bill. You Judas, you surrendered him just like that! But no,
honestly… Do me a favour and shut up, will you, your sort

can't be trusted, that's as clear as Christ walked the earth, until you sent him to his death, that is. What are you talking about? The only one who has sent anyone to their death here is you. Your tongue's too loose, Cain. Now let's see, let me think... leave this Lezama for me to sort out. You just keep your gob shut. I'll be in touch later to let you know what to do. Fine. OK then, now give me the cheques and the blank papers I signed, I've got to get going, things to do. Look, I was thinking I might hold on to the cheques for a bit longer, until this whole mess has cleared up. You'll give me them right now! After I've been to the mortuary. Now! Later! Look, you piece of shit Jew, give me the cheques right now before I send you off to keep your brother company! OK mate. No need to get like that. Everything's fine. Here they are. That's more like it. Now just keep quiet and wait for my instructions. Understood? Understood.

Amancio puts the gun back in the holster and leaves, slamming the door in fury. While he waits for the lift, the neighbour noses quietly through the peephole. Horacio opens the door and pokes his head out.

Amancio. What? I've got to be there at eleven. I'll drop by or call you before that. OK, I'll be waiting.

21

Fuseli has been sitting in the mortuary yard for some time, amusing himself watching the changing skies. It started out as one of those winter days blessed with a little sun. Then later on, typically for this time of year, rain clouds suddenly gathered over the urgent city, an urgency only too evident in the impatient cars jammed up on Viamonte, right outside the mortuary gates. Through those gates comes Lascano, with his familiar bear-like walk. Fuseli smiles: he's always pleased to see his friend. In some way he feels personally responsible for the fact that Lascano's still alive, that Perro was able to overcome the catastrophe of Marisa's death. Fuseli had been Lascano's deep-water harbour, somewhere he could dock until he was ready to set sail again, but set sail where? Fuseli decides he's not in the mood for existential questions today. Right now life consists of him resting in the yard and his friend coming towards him, a friend who owes him a debt, a nice one, one that never need be repaid.

Hey there, Count Dracula. How's the repression going, Perro? Getting better by the day. Did you manage to get me any of that stuff I asked you for? Here you go, I'm told its top-quality Colombian. Is it now? Hmm, it smells like genuine Red Point. Is that any good? Let's find out.

Lascano watches Fuseli's hands as he rolls the weed into a thin Gentleman cigarette paper. His artisan fingers work with agility. He wets the sticky strip with his tongue, finishes sealing it and then twirls a perfect cylinder, smooth and delicate, in his fingertips. He passes it back and forth over the flame of his old Monopol lighter until the dark stain of his saliva disappears. He puts the joint in his mouth and lights up, inhales deeply and holds back a hiccup. The yard fills with an acrid smoke that stings your nostrils. Looking down at the shiny cobbles, Lascano gets the feeling they're at the seaside, fishing.

What the hell, I smoke and you get high? Is it any good? Excellent. Want to try a bit? No thanks. But tell me, why do you smoke that shit? Look, Perro, I spend my days working with death, face to face, you know? Death's the only thing that can't be faked, the only thing you can't falsify or simulate. It's the ultimate truth, and a truth that, what can I say, is not for everyone. So I need to take a break from it all sometimes and this is my break. A little joint and I pick myself up again. It's true that it does fuzz the head a little, but it stimulates your imagination. Basically, we all need an anaesthetic in life, and this is mine. And while we're on the subject, I've been meaning to ask you, what's yours? Me, mate, I live without an anaesthetic, but there is something I want to tell you. Tell me then. A few days ago I organized a raid on a brothel up north. Uh-huh. Well, in the end we'd caught everyone, except for a couple of fish we had to throw back in the water, and I was left wandering about the house to see what I could find. And what did you find? A girl, hiding under a table. And? I nearly died of shock, the girl's identical to Marisa. Ah, so your hallucinating condition is getting serious. I thought it was a vision at first too. But no, it's just that she's identical. She is? She is. I thought I was going mad. *And so what did you do? What could I do? I wasn't even sure if she was real or a ghost. Think about it, I couldn't arrest her but nor could I turn her out on to the street. So I took her home. This is getting good, and so? So nothing, she's there now. Living with you? Yes. You've got to be kidding me! The other night I fucked her, well, she fucked me. And? I don't know, my head's a mess: I don't know whether to shit or wind my watch. You're in love. I don't know, who knows, I don't think so, what does it look like to you? That you're a lost cause. What do you know about her? This is the worst part. Yesterday I found out that she was part of a People's Revolutionary Army cell that just got broken up. And how did she end up in the brothel? I've no idea. Haven't you asked her? No, not just that, I don't want to know. You're scared. I am. I'm telling you, you crazy fool, you're in love. You reckon? I don't reckon, I know. So what shall I do? Infatuation is a passing psychosis, but love is eternal, while it lasts. If you were a true coward, you'd run, but as you're not, you've no choice but to gamble, even though you know you're going to lose. Now you've lost me. It doesn't matter, life's providing you with a respite in the arms of... What did you say her name was? Eva. Eva, well, in her arms. Go with the flow, spin the wheel, you might even get another go. But she's suspected of running with the guerrillas. Right now we're all suspected of something. She's on the run. Who knows she's with you? Only you. Keep it that way. And do what? Enjoy her while you can. And Marisa? Marisa's dead. Has the ghost been back? Now that you mention it, no, she hasn't appeared since Eva's arrival. Now the ghost is Eva. But you really can't imagine how much they resemble one another. Try to focus on the differences, amuse yourself that way. The truth is I envy you. It's been a long time since a woman made my hair stand on end, I think I've dried up. I don't know what to suggest. You don't have to suggest anything. I'll introduce you to her, when you see her you'll fall flat on your arse in disbelief. Oh don't you worry about me. Anyway, I've loads to tell you about Biterman so come on, let's go inside.*

With a sharp yank, Fuseli uncovers the corpse, which now has stitching splitting it in two down the breast bone.

They killed the guy somewhere else, and I would say between seven and nine hours before you found him. Generally speaking, hypostasis becomes fixed between fifteen and eighteen hours after death, but in this case there were blood deposits in several different areas, a clear sign that the body was moved. That's conclusive. He was shot with a nine, from a distance of three to five feet. The bullet entered through the stomach and followed a fairly typical trajectory, passing through the skin, muscle layers, peritoneum, intestine, and finally lodging itself in the pancreas. Here's the bullet. I'll send it to ballistics, but I can tell you now that the gun and entry wound have nothing in common with the other two bodies. This guy was shot at an angle of forty-five degrees, more or less, from shoulder height. The other two were shot straight on, from the front. We recovered three bullets from each of them. They were shot at almost point-blank range in the place where they were found, hypostasis was constant and well fixed. In both their cases, injuries were sustained to the brain and cerebral white matter, death was instant. Biterman must have been alive for a little while after being shot. I don't think I'd be wrong to suggest he attacked his assailant. Look at his hands, these abrasions are typical of those sustained in a fight, but there's no trace of anything similar anywhere else on his body. He does have a few knocks, but as there is no haemorrhaging, it's clear that he received them after death, when he was moved. Here's a detail: we found skin remains under the fingernails, the killer is blood type O negative. What else? They actually did him a favour by killing

142

him. Why? The guy had advanced liver cancer. He would have died soon anyway. They saved him his suffering. That doesn't make the killer any less of a killer. Conclusion? Your suspicions were right. The bullet wounds, types of injury and other marks on the bodies indicate that the kids were executed on the spot while Biterman died in a fight elsewhere. Your murderer should have a fair few scratches on him. Another detail, Biterman had been shot before. How? It must have happened many years ago, but he's got an old gunshot wound in the back, bullet passed through his lung and missed his heart by five millimetres. He was saved by pure luck. Looks like his luck finally ran out.

The door opens and an orderly announces that Horacio has arrived. Fuseli quickly covers the body back up. As Horacio enters, Lascano notices he's wearing brand-new clothes.

This is Doctor Fuseli. Are you ready to identify the body? I'm ready.

Fuseli and Lascano deliberately stand on one side of the table, across from Horacio on the other, the better to monitor his reaction. Fuseli distracts him, Lascano watches him.

I must warn you, Mr Biterman, that what you're about to see is not pleasant. Are you sure you're ready? Yes.

With a flamboyant gesture, Fuseli unveils the body. Horacio goes into some kind of stupor. He covers his mouth with his hand, lowers his head and sobs without much conviction. Lascano and Fuseli exchange sceptical looks.

Elías, what have they done to you? Do you recognize this as the body of your brother, Elías Biterman? Yes. It's him. OK, well, there are some papers you need to sign. When will he be turned over to me?… I need to arrange the funeral. That depends on the judge. More tests are required to determine the time and place of death. Thank you, doctor. Not at all. Lascano, don't go off with my medicine. I won't. Now there's a few questions I need to ask you...

Perro takes Horacio by the arm and leads him out into the courtyard.

Where are you thinking of burying him? He always wanted to be cremated. I understand. Aren't you interested in knowing how he died? Of course I am... It's just that I'm so overcome, everything has been so sudden... Of course. Tell me, you're his only heir, is that correct? If there's anything to inherit, then I suppose I am. Your brother was a moneylender, wasn't he? I imagine that line of work required him being a bit unfriendly to certain clients. Elías was very careful: he never loaned without guarantees. I imagine that on more than one occasion he'll have had to enforce those guarantees. I suppose so. What do you mean you suppose so? You worked with him, surely you know. He handled all that side of things on his own. I just used to run his errands. Like what? Fetch and carry, pay things in at the bank, that sort of thing. What are you thinking of doing now? Well, it's a bit too soon to say. I have to settle my brother's affairs first. Then we'll see. Can you provide me with a list of all his clients? All of them? Just the ones who owed him money. I'll see if I can dig something out.

Horacio departs, Lascano noting that the soles of his shoes are brand new.

22

Hello... Hi Amancio, how's it going... Who's Horacio?...
Who?... Lezama you say?... When?... And what did he say
to him?... I don't understand how this can have happened...
And what does he know?... And what does he know about
me?... OK... No. Don't do anything. Leave it to me ... Yes...
I'll call you... I said leave it to me, you civilians can't be trusted
with anything... Just keep your mouth shut, don't even leave
the house unless I tell you to, understood?

Giribaldi furiously slams the receiver down. It bounces
and falls to the floor, ululating. His mad anger abruptly
subsides and calm restraint takes over. He slowly bends
down, picks up the receiver and replaces it carefully on
the base. He sits motionless for a few minutes. In his
head he goes through the names of the people he'll
have to lean on to sort out the mess that Amancio the
imbecile has caused. "Life on a plate" they used to call
him. Giribaldi's from a lower-middle-class background
and deep down he's always despised Amancio. He finds
him too soft and clumsy, and without a single aim in
life. Giribaldi sees himself as the product of hard
work and endeavour, earning everything through self-
sacrifice, while everything of Amancio's came from
above. Wealth, social standing, his wife, other women,
property, everything for free. With one simple call to

his friend Jorge, Giribaldi finds out that the policeman sticking his nose into the Biterman affair is not called Lezama but Lascano. He also finds out that the bodies have ended up at the mortuary and that the name of the doctor who did the report is one Antonio Fuseli. Giribaldi decides it would be opportune to pay this Fuseli a visit.

From the Lavalle entrance of the Palace of Justice, Giribaldi goes down into the basement, where the Forensic Medical Corps is based. The receptionist makes no comment as he walks past without stopping to explain himself. He marches straight into Fuseli's office without knocking and finds the doctor submerged under a pile of papers. When Giribaldi fires off a "good morning", Fuseli peers at him over his reading glasses, surprised that anyone should so brazenly barge in.

Yes? Doctor Fuseli? That's me. I'm Major Giribaldi. Pleased to meet you, how can I help? I'm led to believe that you're handling the case of three subversives who were killed in a confrontation by the Riachuelo. Three subversives? The case Superintendent Lascano's investigating. Oh, you mean Biterman and the two John Does. Correct. Well, what do you need? To see your report. Unfortunately, just a few moments ago, it was sent to the judge in charge of the case. Which judge? Justice Marraco, his office is on the top floor. Tell me the details. The truth is, Major, with all due respect, you'll have to ask him for that information; if he wants to give it to you, there's no objection on my part.

Giribaldi sits down in front of Fuseli. They don't stop weighing one another up for an instant. They don't say a word and don't move an inch. Fuseli breaks the silence.

Can I help you with anything else? Yes. Do you know Superintendent Lascano? I do. What's your opinion of him?

146

If there were more policemen like him, the force would be a lot better for it. And yet, I've done a little investigating and it seem he's not too well liked by his superiors. As I said, if there were more policemen like him... Is he a friend of yours? I know his work. No more than that? What more do you want to know? He's suspected of having leftist views. These days half the country's suspected of that. You included? Oh I don't know, I'm old enough to stick to the middle ground. Neither the left nor the right fool me. Don't you agree that the times call for us to close ranks on subversion? Major, would you like me to be frank? Please do be. Well, you're going about the guerrilla problem all wrong. Oh really? Yes. You've approached it purely from a military perspective and, as you've all the apparatus of the state at your disposal, you'll no doubt win the battle. And so? But you'll have won by the wrong methods and means. Forgive my frankness. You're forgiven, but please do go on, I'm interested in your position. You ignore the causes which give rise to the guerrilla movement and simply attack the symptoms, and with the most short-sighted methodology I've ever seen. And what would these causes be? The cause is the people, Major. The more deprived people are, the more leftist they are. Why? Because the left promises to share the wealth among many. No matter how little actually does get shared, the poor will always be better off than they were before. Those who have nothing have everything to gain, those who have everything always run the risk of losing it. Think about the barbarians. What about the barbarians? They had no interest in possessions, in owning houses, castles, treasures. That would have meant having to settle somewhere and waste their energies defending their properties. All they wanted to do was attack, rape, pillage and burn. But people aren't barbarous, they will always try to protect their own interests. If you don't let them have anything, then they are barbarians, but as soon as they get some kind of standing, they become bourgeois. So: need draws people to the left, satisfaction to the right. The truth is I don't quite follow you. Basically, Major, it's a problem that needs tackling on two different fronts. One is the armed enemy, who you attack with laws and justice and, if necessary, with force. The other is the people. For rebellion not to take root, you have to give the people things they value, that they can get hold of and that they would want to defend. People aspire to no more than living well, eating every day, educating their children and going on holiday once in a while. It seems to me like you mix everything up. Well, everything is mixed up. Can't you see there's no time for all this theorizing? Now is the time for action. Time, it's precisely the time factor that you're not taking into account. Now you come at me with time? Yes, time passes, situations change and the mistakes you're making now will eventually blow up in your faces. You have some very strange ideas. That's true. And very dangerous. I admit it, there's nothing more risky than being right in a world where everyone else is wrong. But I've long become accustomed to it. Look, doctor, I don't have your education, but there's one thing I'm sure of, that what the communists propose is not what I want for my children. Do you have children? No... Yes. Well either you do or you don't? Yes, one. You're very lucky, I lost mine many years ago and I haven't stopped missing him for a moment. But at least I was able to bury my child. I often get to thinking about all those mothers and fathers whose children are being killed and disappeared. What must their lives be like, how do they manage to overcome their pain? I can tell you from experience, the death of a child is something you never forget. What do you mean by telling me that? Nothing, pay no attention to me, it's just the sense of loss that never leaves a father. Anyway, Major, if that's everything then I'd better get on with my work.

Giribaldi jumps to his feet, as if obeying an order. The forensic doctor's words have confused him. He hates feeling confused. But the feeling will soon turn to anger, and anger, he finds, puts everything back in perspective. Ridiculously, he clicks his heels together and only just stops himself from bowing. Much to his regret, the "good day" he offers in farewell chokes in his throat and comes out timidly. He turns and leaves. Fuseli gets a shiver down his spine. The intimidation that emanates from the man lingers, floating in the air like the smell of steak being cooked on the grill.

Fuseli spends all morning trying to locate Lascano on the phone, but can't get hold of him.

23

Waiting to see the manager, Lascano amuses himself
watching the comings and goings at the bank. He's been
here before. A year ago he was called in to investigate
an inside job involving the then manager and treasurer.
The guys pulled off the perfect fraud. One Monday
morning, they didn't show up for work. Central office
grew increasingly concerned as midday approached
until finally they sent a supervisor to open the safe.
It was empty. They reported the matter immediately.
An expert accountant arrived and calculated that five
million dollars were missing. The investigation got
underway and it was soon established that on Saturday
afternoon the two employees had left the country in a
hired car via the Puente del Inca-Caracoles road, but
there the trail ended. Before the ink had even dried on
their international arrest warrants, the pair sheepishly
handed themselves in to the *Carabineros* in Santiago de
Chile. With due speed, they were flown back to Buenos
Aires and taken, handcuffed, straight from Ezeiza
airport to appear before a judge. They both expressed
their remorse to his honour, saying that temptation had
got the better of them but, having had a chance to think
things through, they realized they had done wrong. To

prove as much, they gladly revealed where they'd hidden the booty. The millions were recovered by a warrant officer, accompanied by half a dozen police officers and led by Lascano. Taking everything into consideration, the thieves were given a short, suspended sentence and were back at large within forty days. They lost their jobs, of course. Lascano noticed that the bank executives didn't seem at all satisfied when they received the recovered cash. It didn't take him long to find out why.

A certain Fermín González worked at the bank, someone Lascano knew had a bit of a murky past. Before Lascano had even threatened to reveal his police record to his employers, Fermín suggested they talk outside and told him straight away what had really happened. There'd not been five million dollars in the safe but fifteen. However, the other ten belonged to a parallel trading desk. The executives had no way of justifying their off-the-balance-sheet activity. The manager and treasurer had seen an opportunity to get their hands on the dirty cash without risk of reprisal. Fermín concluded that if he'd been in their shoes, he'd probably have done the same, after all *who's the bigger thief, the unfaithful employee or the bank?* Perro shrugged his shoulders and offered him a word of advice.

Look, Fermín, maybe you're not aware, but killing has a market value just like any other service. Do you know what the street price is for bumping someone off? No idea. Five hundred dollars for a first-class professional service. So if the opportunity does present itself one day, think about that too.

And here's Fermín now, on the straight and narrow. When he sees Lascano, he smiles and taps his finger to his temple. A secretary then calls for Lascano to go through to see Mr Giménez, the bank manager.

Pleased to meet you. Likewise. What brings you here? I'm investigating a client of yours. Who are we talking about? Elías Biterman. Is he in trouble? He's my trouble now. He's been killed. You're joking? I'm not. Well, you do know I can't give out information on clients without a judicial order. If you insist, then I can get one. But I'm worried that if I don't hurry the killer will get away. I don't need anything written for the moment. All I'm asking for is recent account activity, off the record.

Giménez clears his throat and then leans over to the intercom.

Graciela, bring me Mr Biterman's statements would you please?

The manager adopts a tone of confidentiality.

Well, I can assure you that a lot of people are going to be pleased by this news. So I gather. Between you and me, Biterman was a vampire.

Gracicla brings in the file.

Do you need anything else? That's all thanks.

He waits for the secretary to leave, opens the folder, puts his glasses on and starts to read.

Now let's see… he had a balance of around seventy million… A tidy little sum. If he had that much kept here with us, I can only imagine how much he had tucked away elsewhere… Lately he paid in several cheques, which bounced, adding up to fourteen million pesos in total. Who's were they? Amancio Pérez Lastra's.

Giménez turns the printout around to face Lascano and reaches for a notepad and pencil.

There you go, you can jot the details down while I'm not looking.

Lascano scribbles down the client's name and address, tears the page from the pad and pops it in his pocket.

What else is there? The rest is just cash deposits and withdrawals, bank charges and other such things. Nothing of any significance. Well, thanks, it's been very useful. If I can help you with anything else... Now that you mention it, maybe you can. I've been thinking about getting a safe deposit box. I've a few personal items that I'd like to put out of harm's way. Of course.

Just as before, the manager coughs, leans forward and speaks into the intercom.

Graciela, the Superintendent would like a safe deposit box. Open him an account immediately, would you please. Then bring the forms in and I'll countersign them myself.

Giménez gets up from his chair and walks Perro to the foyer.

Can I authorize my niece to use it? Of course you can. Just tell Graciela and she'll take care of it. You're very efficient. Why thank you.

Within a few minutes, Graciela opens Lascano an account and equips him with a safe deposit box into which he puts the two bundles of dollars recovered from Tony Ventura's brothel. Further down the line, he'll try to persuade Eva to do something worthy with the cash. For now, there's this Amancio character to consider, someone who owed a stack of money to the dead man. It's a Barrio Norte address and Lascano senses he's on the right track. He decides he'll pay Pérez Lastra a visit and *see what he's got to say for himself.*

24

In the morning, Perro leaves his Falcon with Tito, in charge of the police workshop, to get the clutch sorted. He then boards a clapped-out number sixty-one bus and passes the time watching the world go by out of the window. As soon as the traffic jams worsen, and progress becomes too painful to contemplate, he takes out his little book and flicks through the notes he took the other night in police archives. There before him, in his own clumsy scrawl, is a summary of the police version of Eva's story. Half an hour later, the bus drops him at the gates of the Palais de Glace. The slope on Ayacucho isn't suited to inveterate smokers and so he tackles it slowly and carefully, inhaling as much air as his diminished lungs will allow. He approaches the Alvear Palace Hotel, adorned with flags and busy with official cars carrying people to and fro. The pavement is scattered with small light-blue and white propaganda stickers declaring Argentines to be humane and right: *Los argentinos somos derechos y humanos.* He shakes his head and crosses the street. He heads down Quintana, Guido and Vicente López, on towards a formidable building designed by the architect Alejandro Bustillo. This is where Amancio lives. At the door, dressed in the classic grey uniform of a janitor, he finds a man mopping the footpath. Perro approaches him. The man recognizes Lascano's superior authority without a word being said. As soon as he sees him, he leans on the mop handle and greets Lascano with the servile smile of a tip-hunter.

Good morning. Good morning, tell me, does the Pérez Lastra family live here? Yes sir, third floor. You want me to let you in? Do you know if Mr Pérez Lastra is home? I expect so, I've not seen him so far today and he's no early riser. Unless he's gone to the country, but I doubt that as his station wagon's over there.

The man nods towards the other side of the street. Lascano follows his gaze to where a Falcon Rural is parked, encroaching into the bus-stop bay. Perro crosses the road and the porter goes back to his task. Lascano walks around the car inspecting it at great length. He takes out his notebook and jots down the registration number. At that very moment, Amancio comes out of the building with a package in his hand. Lascano tucks his pad away and watches Amancio throw the bundle down by the driver's seat, climb in and start the engine. A few feet further back, a woman in her eighties slowly gets into a taxi. Perro jogs over, arriving just in time to grab the door as she shuts it, jumps in and waves his police badge.

I'm sorry madam, but this is a police emergency. Follow that Rural please.

The woman's eyes light up.

Like in the movies! I'm sorry for any inconvenience. Don't worry, I'm thrilled, finally some excitement. Are we chasing a killer? Just a suspect. Really? Forgive my curiosity, but what's he suspected of? I'm afraid I can't tell you. Of course, gagging orders. Exactly. Oh my, wait until I tell the girls.

The driver is skilful and soon gets onto the Rural's tail. After a few minutes they reach the junction of Esmeralda and Viamonte. Amancio sticks his hand out of the window to signal he's going into a car park.

Drop me here. Sorry once again madam. Not at all, a pleasure, though nothing much happened in the end.

Lascano puts a couple of notes in the driver's hand, gets out and mixes in with the hustle and bustle of the street. Amancio comes out of the car park, crosses the road and enters the Banco Municipal de Préstamos, the pawnbrokers. Lascano follows him in. Pérez Lastra goes over to a counter and Perro feigns interest in the items on display, positioning himself so that he can comfortably monitor goings on at the desk. Amancio speaks to an attendant, opens his parcel and takes out a nine millimetre. The sales assistant inspects it, asks a question. Amancio nods his head. The attendant puts the pistol in a wooden box and starts to fill out a form. He says something and Amancio immediately takes out his wallet and shows his ID card. The assistant quickly writes the number down and then spins the ledger around and passes over a pen. Amancio signs his name and hands it back. The assistant adds his signature and stamps a seal on four counterfoils. He tears one off, passes it to Amancio and directs him over to the cashier desks. Amancio takes the piece of paper and joins one of the queues, eagerly anticipating his earnings. He weighs up the length of the line then pulls out a copy of the *Palermo Racing Post* and starts reading. Lascano, without letting Amancio out of his sight, goes over to the check-in desk and furtively shows his badge to the attendant.

Tell me, what transaction did the man you just served make? Who, that one?

The assistant raises his hand and points over to Amancio. Lascano quickly grabs his arm and pulls it down.

A little discretion, please. Oh yeah, sorry. The guy deposited a pistol. Let me see it.

The attendant gets out the wooden box and puts it on the counter. Perro picks up the gun and holds the barrel to his nose. The smell of gunpowder is very fresh. The clip is missing. He takes the small piece of plastic that he found in the lift from his pocket and compares it with a chip in the handle. Perfect fit. In his notebook, he copies down the basic details from the ledger. He bids farewell to the employee. Amancio's still standing in the queue. Lascano heads out into the street and hails a taxi.

Palermo racecourse, please.

Lascano stations himself near the entrance to the grandstand gallery. Fifteen minutes later, Amancio enters with all the airs and graces of the Shah of Persia and heads for the café. Lascano allows himself a smug smile. He waits for a moment, then follows. He finds Amancio sitting at a table in the company of a young woman, beautiful and distant, with the self-assurance of the well-bred girl, for whom everything seems the most natural thing in the world. Too conscience, perhaps, of how attractive she is. Perro sits down by the window, from where he can watch them without being noticed. A familiar face approaches their table. Everyone greets one another and they speak briefly. The loudspeaker announces the start of the third race. Horacio excuses himself and leaves. Amancio studies the race programme and Lara looks bored. Out of the window, Lascano sees Horacio, down by the fence that separates the track

158

from the public. *Time to get this show on the road,* Perro says to himself, and heads over to the Pérez Lastras. He flashes them his badge and sits down at their table.

Good day. Good day. I'm Superintendent Lascano. Are you Mr Pérez Lastra? The very same. This is my wife, Lara. Nice to meet you. How can I be of help? I'm conducting an investigation into an associate of yours and need to ask you a few questions. Ask away. Elías Biterman. Biterman? Yes, of course, I know Biterman. What's your relationship with him? Commercial. He cashes cheques for me or lends me modest sums. Do you owe him much money? I believe I do owe him a little, yes. When was the last time you saw him? Is the Yid in trouble? Answer my question please. I don't know, it would be about a week ago. Where did you meet him? In a café on Florida. Do you remember which one? The Richmond. What was the purpose of the meeting? To sort out the payments I owe him. How much do you owe him? Well, I don't have the figures with me. Approximately. I don't know, a million, more or less. And what arrangements did you come to? In the end, none at all. It was left that he was going to send me the bill with an invoice through his brother, Horacio, but he never did. So I see. Can you tell me where you were on Tuesday night? Tuesday? We ate at home, isn't that right dear? Err yeah. Yes, we went to bed early. How did you injure your head? I fell off my horse out in the country. Do you have a car? Yes. A Falcon Rural 74. What colour? Grey. Where is it? Here, in the club car park. Do you want to see it? That won't be necessary. What blood group are you? O negative. Would you mind telling me what this is all about? Biterman was murdered. What? Like you heard. You don't think that... I don't think anything yet. I'm talking to all his debtors. I see. Well, that's everything. I may have to speak to you again. Good day, sir, sorry to disturb you. ... Good day.

Lascano stands up and performs a little bow before leaving.

And what shit have you got yourself mixed up in now, darling? Nothing, it seems that someone I know has been killed. I heard that bit, was it you? But how can you even think such a thing? On Tuesday I got back at seven in the morning and you weren't home. I've already explained that to you. Yes, you explained it to me, but you just lied about it to the police.

25

It's a clear morning. Giribaldi sits impatiently at the wheel of his car. He's wondering what's taking Maisabé so long, given that she said she was ready to leave when he went to get the car from the garage. Finally she appears, carrying the baby as if she's concealing a secret. Giribaldi opens the back door. He looks in the rear view mirror and sees that her face is strained, and she's been crying. *What is up with her?* He decides to go the bottom way. He takes 9 de Julio, turns onto Diagonal Norte and continues down towards Casa de Gobierno. A group of mothers-of-the-disappeared are congregated in Plaza de Mayo, doing circuits around the pyramid-shaped monument, wearing white handkerchiefs on their heads.

Maisabé fixes her eyes on these silent women, as the car skirts around them on Hipólito Yrigoyen. The traffic lights on Defensa halt their progress. They come to a stop, right across from the women. One of them stops her march and stares at Maisabé, who feels like she's been discovered. The woman walks towards the car with a hard look on her face. Fear grips hold of Maisabé's throat, her muscles tense and she doesn't realize she's squeezing the child too tightly. The baby starts crying.

Giribaldi asks what the matter is. A horn sounds behind them, the lights change, he slips into first and pulls away. Maisabé looks around and sees the mother by the cordon now, greeting and embracing another woman. Maisabé begins to tremble and weep.

Can you please tell me what on earth you're crying for? No reason, Leonardo, it's nothing, just leave me be.

They carry on along Leandro Alem heading north, with no option but to join the typically chaotic morning traffic. Giribaldi comes to a stop outside The Horse café, under the train tracks, on the corner of Avenida Juan B. Justo and Libertador. He leaves his wife and child to wait in the car and goes into the café, where Amancio sits at a table, anxiously stirring his coffee. *A weak and contemptible being, always preoccupied with his wife, a whore no matter how many barrels to her name. Always begging, always drowning in a glass of water, although in his case it would have to be a glass of whisky. It's always the same with civilians, more doubt than strength of will.* Giribaldi approaches Amancio's table but remains standing, the better to emphasize his stature, his superiority. Amancio offers up what he believes to be his best smile.

Giri, it looks like this thing's gone from bad to worse. Now what? A policeman came to see me. He asked me loads of questions about Biterman. Lascano? That's him. You stupid fool. Last time you told me his name was Lezama and I had to bust my arse finding out who it really was. I said Lezama? Yes. Sorry, I was mistaken. You're always mistaken. What you now have to get into your head is that you've got yourself involved in a game with the big boys, where errors are paid for dearly. You're right, and I'm sorry. Stop saying sorry all the time, won't you? What did Lascano want? It's the same guy who went to see Horacio. No shit! What did you tell him? Nothing, but he

162

asked me hundreds of questions. The guy suspects something. How did he get to you? How do I know? Would Horacio have told him? I don't know, maybe. Does he know anything about me? Who? Horacio, who else? Not a thing. You sure? Come on, do you take me for a complete fool? Well, the truth is that you are a bit of a fool.

Giribaldi looks up and sees Maisabé standing by the car, clutching the baby, rocking it nervously as it waves its hands about and bawls. Amancio assumes himself responsible for the look of anger that spreads over Giribaldi's face.

Right. I've got to go and see this priest you recommended, see if he can cure Maisabé of the craziness she's got with the kid. And what about me, what shall I do? You grab that little whore of yours, lock up your house and head out to the country, and you do it right now, and you stay there until I tell you otherwise. And whatever happens, keep your trap shut. If they nab you, let me know straight away. Tell them that for security reasons you have to inform Major Giribaldi. Is that clear? Crystal.

26

Waiting in the sacristy, Maisabé rocks the baby frantical-ly, not realizing it's fallen asleep. Giribaldi kills time looking at the depictions of suffering hanging on the wall. The Sacred Heart, wrapped in its crown of thorns, drips blood on the world. To one side, Saint Sebastian, pierced with arrows, endures martyrdom with a bit of a poof's expression on his face. Next to him, Saint George, ferocious, skewers the dragon, which writhes on the ground at the horse's feet. Father Roberto opens the door. He's young, wears jeans and a T-shirt and could easily pass for an engineering or economics student. He has a wide, childish smile and a deliberate, somewhat affected manner. He speaks gently.

Major, what a pleasure, and you must be Maisabé. And the little one, what's he called? His name's Aníbal, Father. No need to call me father, my name's Roberto. As you wish. Now what is it that's bothering you?

Roberto notices that Maisabé seems apprehensive in the presence of Giribaldi, who looks like he's keeping watch over a dangerous prisoner.

Major, you wouldn't be offended if I asked for a moment alone with your wife? What? No, no, of course not, I'll wait outside. Many thanks...

The Major wavers a second and then leaves, as if going to do his penance.

OK, now tell me, Maisabé, what's troubling you? I don't know if you know, Father... sorry, Roberto, but this child is actually... No need to explain, I know all about it. But tell me, what's the matter with you, it doesn't seem like you've taken to motherhood so well. I think I'm going crazy. But why? The child hates me. But how can this little angel hate you? He looks at me in a certain way... In what way? As if he's accusing me of what happened to his mother, of having stolen him from her. But no, you're confusing things, Maisabé, that's all in your imagination. When a child is born it's common for mothers to get a bit flustered. Now you may not have given birth to this child, but you wanted to so much that I think something similar is happening to you. You think so? It seems that way. The other night I became convinced that I was living in sin for having stolen him. You've not stolen anything, Maisabé, you have saved this child. Yes, but the mother... The mother was not capable of protecting him and got herself mixed up in things she shouldn't have. You're not to blame for what happened to her. She's the only one to blame, she ought to have thought better of it before getting mixed up in what she did. But doesn't a person live in sin if they keep stolen goods?

The priest puts his hand over her head then gently takes hold of her chin.

Maisabé!... that's for things, not for people. Think about it a little, what would have become of this poor angel if it had grown up in a subversive household? You have to realize that God intervened to put this child in your hands. Divine Providence was moved to pity the child's destiny and give him a Christian home, where he'll be raised with true values. You and your husband represent those values, and that's why you're here.

Ashamed of what she's about to say, Maisabé bows her head. Roberto's hand lingers on her neck.

Father, the other night I thought about killing him, so as to return him to his mother. Well, I understand you feeling remorse, which shows that you're a good person. Sometimes our best intentions lead us down the wrong path, but you've seen the light and the sin of evil thought is forgiven. Really Father?... Roberto. Of course, Maisabé, come with me...

He directs her towards a prayer bench, where they both kneel. He hands her an image of the Virgin of the Immaculate Conception surrounded by cherubs, hand in the air, eyes looking up to the sky, with her burgeoning belly. He reaches an arm around Maisabé's shoulders and places his other hand, fist clenched, against his breast.

Recite with me the Prayer for Lost Children.

Embraced by Roberto, babe in arms and staring determinedly at the image, Maisabé softly repeats the priest's words.

Oh Lord! with all that you see, watch over this lost child, that has been found.

Oh Lord! with all that you are able, help all children find the path to You.

Oh Lord! may Your infinite piety protect this child.

With your merciful hand, like Moses, lead him through stormy waters.

Give him a pure life, full of You, and for Your great glory.

In the name of the Father, and of the Son and of the Holy Spirit. Amen.

Aníbal, Maisabé, I bless you in the name of God. Go now in peace.

Giribaldi can't believe his eyes when he sees Maisabé come out of the sacristy, closely followed by Roberto.

She seems like she's walking on air, her whole face has changed, become illuminated, serene and harmonious. Her hands hold the little one with loving tenderness and, when she passes Giribaldi's side, she gives him a soft smile, as if from another world. Giribaldi feels, and holds back, a strong urge to cry, which immediately turns to a sense of terror.

Will Maisabé ever return from this other world or is she stuck there for ever?

27

Lascano drops in at the police mechanics workshop and picks up his car. He's been told to present himself before his superior at ten. He plunges into the city's traffic.

His boss is known as Blue Dollar, because even a complete fool can tell how false he is. Lascano wonders what his boss wants. Perro knows he'll have to be very careful. Rumour has it that Blue Dollar sent several policemen into a trap from which no one came out alive. They say that's how he gets people off his back, especially those who stick their nose into his business. Blue Dollar runs a kickback racket linked to the allocation of police jurisdictions. If a superintendent wants to be in charge of a particular police station, he has to pay a price for the keys. Different jurisdictions naturally have different prices. The First is the most valued and sought after. Given its downtown location, it's the one that brings in the most profitable business. It's got everything: bars, nightclubs, whores, traffickers, homosexuals, bankers, businessmen; everyone has something to hide, something they need, something to disguise. All this means a licence to print money. Lascano has always steered clear of the system, never shown any interest in getting involved, which suits him fine, but makes those that are embroiled very suspicious.

Near Congreso, Lascano checks his watch and sees he's right on time. At three minutes to ten he enters police headquarters via the Moreno entrance. He skirts around the courtyard of palm trees, heads up to the second floor and, at ten on the dot, knocks on Blue Dollar's door. The boss has company, someone Lascano immediately sees is military, and an acidic bubble bursts in his stomach.

Good morning, sir. Good morning Lascano, allow me to introduce Major Giribaldi. Pleased to meet you. So you're the famous Perro Lascano. Famous? Everyone knows you. That's not much good in my line of work, I prefer to go about my business unnoticed. I bet you do. Well, Lascano, the Major here has something he needs to talk to you about, so if you'll forgive me, I've a matter to attend to. I'll leave you two here to chat in peace. Whatever you say. Thanks Jorge.

Lascano's boss puts on his cap and the tailored jacket of his uniform and leaves the office. Giribaldi takes his seat behind the desk.

So, what are you up to Lascano? The same as ever, working. What are you working on? A homicide. Biterman. How did you know? I know a lot of things. So I see. You picked up three bodies down by the racetrack. That's right. You took them to the mortuary. Correct. Well, for your information, those bodies were three subversives who did battle with my men. I didn't know that, but one of the bodies caught my attention, Biterman, who was a lot older than the others. Do you think all subversives are twenty years old? No, I've heard that some are fifteen, some twelve, some even as young as one. Are you trying to be funny? Not in the least. I'm just telling you what I know. What else do you know? That Biterman was killed somewhere else and planted

170

with the others. And what's that to you? I'm a policeman. And if you're such a keen policeman, why didn't you investigate the other two bodies? Because I'm not allowed to, as you well know. But at least one of them will get justice. Don't break my balls with talk of justice. In these times, we can't afford to be fooling around. I'm telling you that you can't investigate Biterman either. Understood? Is that an order? It's an order...

The military man studies the policeman in silence, his fists tightly clenched on the desk. He lets out a sigh and reclines in his seat.

You see, Lascano, you're an estimable guy, a smart cop. But there are some things you just don't seem to get. Like what? Oh never mind, I'm not going to start explaining now. Just stop messing around with this case and forget about this piece of shit Jew. You've a lot more to lose than to gain from it. Really? Look, I'll make you an offer. Come and work for me. I'll improve your rank and salary. But first take a nice long holiday with that girlfriend you've got kept at home. I'd prefer to stick where I am. Not accepting what I'm offering you would be very stupid, and I don't think you're stupid. So stop messing about, Lascano, and do as you're told. It'll suit you. I'll have to think about it. You think about it... but not for too long. You wouldn't happen to be a lefty, would you? A lefty? No, I try to abide by rights in everything I do. That sort of sarcasm is going to be your downfall one day. I want an answer by tomorrow. Tell Jorge and I'll contact you. All right, anything else? You can go. Thanks, good day.

Perro doesn't wait around for the lift, descending the stairs at full pelt. The bubble in his stomach turns into a fireball. He fears he's going to be picked up at the very door to police headquarters. He strides out to the street corner, jumps in his car and pulls away. Two blocks on, he puts his flashing light on the roof and crosses the city like a demon, without stopping at a single traffic light, snaking through the crazy morning traffic and not even lighting a single cigarette the whole journey. When he gets home, he parks any old place, without even wasting time on locking the door. He bursts into the apartment like a whirlwind.

At that same moment, two men, one tall and well-built, with a good beer belly, the other short, grey-haired and skinny, enter the Bitermans' building. They get to the fourth floor just as Horacio comes out of his door carrying a suitcase. They address him by his name and when he replies that yes, it's him, Grey pulls out a pistol and puts a bullet in his head. Horacio's shoes are left where he was standing, but he goes on a brief flight, ending when his head smashes into the wall and his body spills to the floor, eyes open. A torrent of blood immediately starts to pour out of him. When the echoes of the gunshot die out, Beer Belly catches the sound of the neighbour shutting the spyhole. Grey motions with his head. Belly goes over to the neighbour's door, takes out his gun and cocks it. He rings the bell. The peephole shutter slides open and the neighbour's voice asks who's there. Belly puts the barrel of his gun into the little window and pulls the trigger. On the other side, the sound of the neighbour's body falling to the floor is heard. When Belly turns around, Grey is already waiting in the lift. Belly catches him up and they leave.

Lascano slams the door, making Eva jump out of her skin.

Ehh, what's going on? Girl, I've no time to explain. We have to leave right away. Where to? I'll explain later. Get a bag together with our things. Essentials only. Don't forget documents. But what's happened? Just trust me. I'll explain later. There's no time now. We have to leave right now. OK.

Eva's reaction is immediate and extremely efficient. She quickly finds and gathers what's most important. The experience of several years' clandestine existence means she knows the order of priorities, the order to pack the bag. But she hates the return of this dizzy fleeing feeling. While she concentrates on her task, Lascano picks up the phone.

Yes... Doctor Fuseli please... come on, come on.... yes, Doctor Fuseli... Hello, yes, Fuseli?... Perro... Bad, all bad... The cat's out the bag... Really, when? Well, I know it's my trail they're on, but it'd be no surprise if they came after you too. It looks like the whole thing's taken a very dark turn... Of course they must know, and even if they don't, they'll be finding out as we speak... I think the game's up... I'm leaving right now... Not at all... Take them now... Have you got anywhere to go?... That's fine, don't tell me... You got cash?... OK... Yes, but I mean right now, you got it? Straight away... Good luck... Bye... and sorry to have mixed you up in this mess... Thanks... Bye... take care.

Eva holds the bag in one hand, the door open with the other.

All ready? Ready. Let's go.

They hurry out. Lascano stops.

What's up? We're forgetting something. What?

Perro turns on his heels and goes over to the birdcage. He opens the lid and takes the bird out carefully in his hand, goes over to the window, opens it and lets it loose.

I had to let it go free, otherwise it would've starved to death. You're such a sentimentalist, but I love you for it.

The house is quiet. The bird stands with its tiny claws on the balcony handrail. From nowhere, fast as lightning, a cat jumps out, grabs the bird in its paws and sinks its fangs into its head, making the skull *crack* like a nut.

173

28

Wood pigeons flutter in the eucalyptus trees. It's a splendid morning. Winter has yet to completely dull the brilliant symphony of autumn ochres. Amancio is sitting on the porch at La Rencorosa, dressed in his baggy country trousers, espadrilles, gaucho shirt and suede jacket, with a red handkerchief tied around his neck. He's feeling relaxed for the first time in ages and entertains himself reading the obituaries in *La Nación*. All he has to do is sit and wait until the whole Biterman business blows over. Giribaldi will put the cop in his place and then Amancio will be able to get back to handling his affairs in the city. He plans to light the barbecue with the cheques and guarantees he signed for Biterman.

When he's out in the country, a rural feeling takes control of him, even the way he talks. At his side, Lara, as usual, is polishing her nails. As far as she's concerned, the countryside is a dreadful place where live chickens wander about and, in protest, she dresses and dolls herself up as if she were going shopping in Santa Fe. She doesn't understand why they have to be out there. Amancio hasn't really explained the situation, as he fears she'll use it against him one day. Doña Lola comes out of the kitchen with the implements for the *mate* and places them on the little table between them. Lara finds *mate* disgusting.

I don't know how you can drink that filth. I like it, dear, don't forget that I'm a man of the country. Then why don't you stay and live out here, you and your chickens?

He ignores the comment and enjoys the simple pleasure of having her here with him, in a sense captive, with no place she can go, with no possibility of meeting up with the Pole, Ramiro or whoever else. Along the road that leads to the ranch, a breeze swirls the fallen leaves into the air. Amancio looks up. Down by the gate, a Ford Falcon has arrived with two men inside. No further details are required to determine they're Giribaldi's people. They've doubtless come to tell Amancio that everything has been sorted out. He calls Doña Lola and tells her to go and open the gate for them. He gets to his feet and adopts his best master-of-the-ranch pose. The woman hurries down the drive, mechanically drying her hands on a dishcloth as she goes. The car comes in and pauses as it passes Doña Lola, the driver speaking to her briefly. She stays down by the gate, without closing it. The car gets to the porch, the man in the passenger seat gets out, walks around the back of the car and stands five paces away from Amancio. Lara has hitched up her skirt a few inches so that the visitors can admire her magnificent legs.

Mr Amancio Pérez Lastra? At your service. I imagine Giribaldi sent you. That's right. Well, what's the message?

In reply, the man pulls out a pistol and fires. A flock of pigeons goes into flight, abandoning the formidable branches of the eucalyptus. Amancio topples over, dragging down the thermos flask, the *mate* and the cruet set holding the sugar and the *yerba*. Lara's paralysed, her bottom jaw left hanging, her pretty face glazed over in stupid astonishment. The killer points the barrel at her and shoots. With the force of the impact, Lara's head makes a circular movement and her lovely hair whirls about as if in a shampoo commercial, then she falls, along with her seat and everything else, down into the geraniums. The killer goes over to the dead bodies and fires point-blank into each of their temples. He heads back to the car, which the driver has already spun around to face the exit, gets in and off they go. At the gate, Doña Lola, terrified, immobile, pale as a ghost, clutches the dishcloth. The Falcon drives up alongside her and halts, the driver sticks a gun out of the window, she raises the dishcloth as if it were a shield. The man shoots her through the cloth and then, as she lies sprawled in a clump of clover, he finishes her off with another bullet. The car drives through the gate and heads back to wherever it came from.

The warbling of the birds slowly returns, the wind plays with the leaves, the wood pigeons fly back to their nests and the dust clouds left by the visitors gently settle.

29

*Girl, everything has gone sour with a case I'm on. What
happened? I started to investigate a murder and it led me right
into the military pigsty. You're kidding? I wish I was. Lascano,
you know that I... You don't have to tell me anything, girl, I
know all about you. And? And it doesn't change anything. If
I was your age I'd probably do the same. Do what? Try to kick
these sons of bitches out of power before they've run us all into
the ground. Lascano, you never cease to surprise me. Well, right
now we need to leave the country before we get a nasty surprise
from them. So what's the plan? Look, I have to close this case.
Don't ask me why. So first I'm going to leave all the evidence
with the judge. What for? So that my job's done. You're such a
dreamer, Lascano. I do my job. And then? I hand this in, then
we go to the bank to withdraw the dollars we found at Ventura's
and from there head straight to the airport and catch the first
flight to Iguazu. Cross the triple frontier in one step. After that,
wherever you want to go. Brazil? Brazil. Bahia? Bahia.*

Lascano parks the car next to the Lavalle monument.
He sticks a police sign on the windscreen and runs
across Tucumán, zigzagging between the buses. He
disappears for a second, lost in the swarming sea of
lawyers. He reappears on the steps leading up to the
Palace of Justice and then disappears again between the

columns. Eva feels her heart shrink. She puts on a pair of Ray Bans she finds in the glove compartment.

Marraco's busy attending a hearing. Lascano sits down on a bench in the corridor facing the patio and waits. He looks down at the group of cells where they put defendants brought in to appear in court. The accused anxiously wait to be called, to be taken handcuffed to the courtroom to learn their fate, given their freedom or find out they really are in the shit. The prisoners are nervous and impatient in the circumstances and pace back and forth in their cells, taciturn and absorbed in thought. As a result, the place is known as the Lion's Den: *La Leonera*. Perro sits very still on the bench, but inside he too feels like a caged lion. He has to wait for an hour before the judge's office boy gives him the signal to come through. Marraco is sitting at his desk, looking refined as ever, but is noticeably disgruntled with the mountain of resolutions, orders, sentences and decrees he has to sign, instead of being out playing golf. Lascano throws a manila envelope on top of the file that Marraco's reading.

What's this? The Biterman case. It's solved. Well, how very efficient. If all police officers were like you... Fill me in. Amancio Pérez Lastra is the murderer. He killed him because he owed him loads of money. Biterman, the victim, defended himself. Amancio has injuries on his face and deposits of his skin were found under the nails of the corpse. Aha. Horacio was his accomplice. The little brother? How nice, a game of happy families. And now for the best part. Go on. The body was planted by the Riachuelo, alongside two kids Giribaldi's group shot. For some reason, the Major decided he would send for the bodies to be moved later. In the meantime, a lorry driver came across them and reported it. I was sent to check things out, but before I arrived Amancio planted Biterman's body there too. So when I got there I found three bodies instead of two. Major Giribaldi gave the details to Amancio so that his people could make the body disappear like a John Doe along with the other two. And you can prove all this? It's all in there. I've found the murder weapon too, a nine millimetre that Pérez Lastra pawned at the Banco de Préstamos, the details are in the folder. Very good Lascano, very good. Leave it all with me. Tomorrow we'll pick up Pérez Lastra. I'll get to work on it right now. Include an order to impound Amancio's car: the body was transported in it and there'll doubtless be traces. It wouldn't be a bad idea to also search his ranch, La Rencorosa, just in case. All the information is in the envelope. Right you are.

All Perro can think about is getting out of there and back to Eva as soon as possible. He makes his excuses and leaves. When he opens the door, he comes face to face with the office junior, who pretends he was just about to come in. The boy offers him a generous smile and Lascano returns the compliment, patting him on the head.

See you, kid, look after yourself.

In the mortuary, Fuseli hastily gathers up his last bits and pieces. From where he's standing, he can keep an eye on the gateway, and he sees a Ford Falcon pull in and two men get out. He knows it's them, that they've come for him. He tucks his bag out of sight, climbs on top of a dissection table and covers himself with a sheet. The guys come in, traipse around the room and then head out, back to the gate. Fuseli sees them talking to the security guard, who directs them off to the right. The killers walk out onto the street and turn in the direction of Junín. Fuseli pulls out his bag and takes his watch from a pocket. He waits a minute, time enough, he calculates, for them to reach the administration office, and goes out.

Chapparo! Yes, doctor? Come here a second. Doctor, some people are looking for you. Yes, I was expecting them, I was wondering where they'd got to. They couldn't find you down here so I thought you must be up in 760. Do me a favour, would you? Go and tell them to come back down. I'll wait for them in the operating room. I'll go and get them now. Thanks.

The guard scurries off. Fuseli runs back in, grabs his bag and then hurries out into the street. He hails the first taxi he sees. When he reaches the corner, he sees Chaparro returning with the two men.

Where to, sir? Retiro station, please.

A few blocks away, Lascano gets back in his car and puts it in gear. Eva looks serene on the surface, but inside she's Krakatoa volcano ready to erupt. Perro breathes deeply and joins the river of tin cans that is the traffic heading towards Tucumán. After a few minutes they pull up outside the bank. Lascano takes a key out of his pocket and gives it to Eva.

What's this? It's the key to a safe deposit box in this bank. Ask for Graciela, tell her you're my niece and that you need to get something. Take out all the Tony Ventura cash. OK, back in a minute.

Eva looks into his eyes and gives him a kiss, lingering an instant, then gets out without saying another word. Lascano watches her go into the bank and head to the counter. He takes out a cigarette and lights it. The fuel gauge shows that Tito and the boys siphoned off all the petrol in the tank: Lascano will have to stop and fill up if they're going to get anywhere. In the bank, Graciela talks to Eva, who turns around towards Lascano and smiles. All is well. Graciela comes out from behind the counter and tells Eva to follow her and they both disappear down a side staircase to the basement, where the treasure's kept.

A traffic warden approaches, confidently fluttering a book of counterfoils in his hand. Lascano takes a deep puff on his cigarette and winds the window down. The warden realizes he's before a superior, without Lascano having to say a word or show any identification. Perro raises his hand towards his chin and wags a finger to tell the warden to move on and ask no questions. The warden walks on by. Lascano watches him amble away in his rear-view mirror. A Falcon turns the corner at top speed. Perro's heart leaps and he instinctively reaches for his shoulder holster. The Falcon pulls up in front of Lascano's car, the doors open, two men jump out, guns in hands, and start shooting at him. Lascano opens the door, dives to the pavement and rolls over, pulling out his gun. People in the street start running or throw themselves to the ground. Lascano jumps up and, pointing his index finger along the barrel, aims at the head of the nearest of the men and shoots. The impact spins the man around. Perro, in quick succession, shoots twice more. The force of the bullets throws the man onto the bonnet of a car, then he bounces off and crashes to the ground like a sack of potatoes. As Lascano takes aim at the second man, he feels like he's been punched in the chest and the blow sits him down on the pavement, behind the open door of his car. The shooter has lost sight of Lascano. He takes two steps to the side, trying to get a clear view in order to deal the killer blow. When he next sees Lascano, the policeman's aiming a gun right between his eyes. Without hesitating, Perro pulls the trigger and sends the little missile right into the middle of the man's forehead. He drops down dead on the pavement, legs shaking in a final spasm. A ferociously sharp pain grips Lascano's chest, his shirt starts to soak with blood, his vision becomes misty, he feels very tired and slumps down on his side in slow motion. Head on the ground, he sees his cigarette on the pavement before him, still smouldering. He slowly reaches out, grabs it, puts it to his mouth and inhales deeply. It suddenly becomes night.

Hell, this hurts.

A curious crowd gathers around Lascano and the two other fallen men. Eva comes out of the bank clutching her purse. She freezes. The traffic warden comes running back, bends down over Lascano's body, puts two fingers to the policeman's neck, searches for a pulse and grimaces in resignation. At that moment a patrolman's gumboots screech to a halt beside him. An officer and a sergeant approach the bodies and look at them as if they were mere things. Two policemen busy themselves dispersing the crowd. Graciela comes out of the bank with other employees to find out what's going on. Graciela sees Lascano on the ground, she seems to recognize him and then looks at Eva, frozen at his side. Eva starts to react and realizes that she needs to leave immediately. She walks to the corner, the opposite direction to where the police are coming from. She stops a taxi, gets in and asks to be taken to the first place that pops into her head, to Rosedal, the rose garden.

Eva sits in front of the monument to Sarmiento and recalls the first lines of the school hymn: *Fue la lucha tu vida y tu elemento, la fatiga tu descanso y calma* – the struggle *was your life and essence, weariness your rest and calm* – and she murmurs them like a lament. She repeats them again and again, mechanically like a mantra, hypnotized, sitting motionless on the bench in the square, her legs frozen. Thus she remains for hours, not noticing the couples who walk by arm in arm, the ducks swimming in the stagnant waters of the lake, the bare wisteria in the pergola, the children bunking off school with their books and their blazers hidden under their coats, the grumpy one-armed municipal caretaker, the adventurers paying twenty pesos for an hour on the strange metal pedalos. Eva spends the rest of the day in this dazed state. When the sun comes down on the racetrack side of the park, she gets up and starts walking. Slowly at first, but then her muscles start to warm up and she picks up her pace. She runs past the Urquiza statue of the war horse, the Planetarium, the bridges over the train tracks. She goes all the way around the Aeropark, heads on to Costanera Avenue, indifferent to the darkened river, and carries on jogging until she reaches the airport, where she buys a ticket on the first flight to Resistencia.

30

The judge's office boy is arranging the case files that Marraco has just signed, readying them for the filing cabinets where they'll be available to lawyers for reference. The judge is rounding off a conversation on the phone.

Yes... no problem... agreed... don't worry about a thing... I'm sure an opportunity will present itself... OK... OK... whenever you like... perfect... we'll be in touch then a pleasure... likewise.

Hey, kid. Yes, Judge. Drop what you're doing and take this envelope to this address. Hurry, they're waiting for it. What about the case files? Tell Marcos to finish them off. Go on, hurry along. Yes, your honour.

Giribaldi takes his time lighting the fire, enjoying every moment of it. At army camp in his youth, he developed a special technique that meant he could get a fire going in the most adverse conditions. Whenever a fire needed preparing, the other cadets at Military College would say, *let Giri light it, let the champion light it.* Because Giri is champion of the flames. Now, even in the comfort of his own home, even in a fireplace, Giribaldi prepares the fire as if he's at camp in Zapala, in the depths of winter, with forty-mile-an-hour winds. He takes pleasure in rolling the newspaper into giant straws and tying them by their ends into hoops. He then lays them one on top of the other to form a pyramid.

He covers them with wood chip and then, concentrically, adds ever bigger chunks. The result of his toils burns away in the hearth. On top of the lively fire he places a hefty branch of a *quebracho* tree, which the flames lick with appetite. The crackle of the wood is like a lullaby to the Major, hypnotized by the dancing tongues of fire. On the flowery armchair, Maisabé nestles the child, with the beatified smile she's had stamped on her face since Father Roberto blessed them. In the kitchen, Sunday's leftover ravioli is slowly reheating in a bain-marie. The doorbell rings. Giribaldi gets up and goes to the door. Maisabé hears him talk briefly with someone, then sees him come straight back in.

Who was it? Just someone bringing me something. Nothing important.

The Major rips open the envelope. There's the photo of Elías Biterman lying dead, the forensics, ballistics and laboratory reports, a long statement signed by Lascano describing the various stages and findings of the investigation. Giribaldi thinks what a shame it is that this cop, such a great investigator, is not on the side of the just. *But well, brilliant minds are often the ones most easily misled. When people get to thinking too much, they usually end up in the shit.* One by one, he throws the documents onto the burning logs and watches, fascinated by the spectacle: the white paper first changes colour, browned by the fire, then, when it hits 451 degrees, it ignites with a little explosion. The flames devour it, blacken it, change its substance, its essence, but it's still possible to make out the writing amidst the dark mass. The heat contorts the paper until the material bearing the words is vaporized, broken up into thousands of particles, some floating up and disappearing, others incorporating themselves into the charred mass, where everything is uniform, where nothing lives, where finally the words die, where all that remains are ashes, inert, sterile, silent, the final remains of the facts, a hymn to purification. Blank and clear once more, as blank now as nothing.

Eva's ears sense the moment the aeroplane doors close. Out of the window, the bus that brought the passengers to the stairway pulls away and heads back to the terminal. The mechanics move away from the plane talking distractedly among themselves and the signalman directs the aircraft as it manoeuvres itself towards the runway. Eva feels strange. She's always been scared of flying, but now, as the chassis bumps over the gaps in the paving, she doesn't feel anything, no fear at all. As the plane files past the tall trees and traffic on the adjacent Avenida Costanera, watching the office workers on their way home, she feels empty in the absence of fear. She thinks about how it wouldn't matter to her in the least if the plane crashed and she died along with all these strangers surrounding her.

As this is happening, not so very far away, Marcelo, the court office boy, has shut himself away in his room at his parents' house. The shelves on the bookcase warp under the weight of all the books he has to digest to become a lawyer. On his lap he has an envelope full of photocopies that he's paid for out of his own pocket. He pulls one out and starts reading: *From: Superintendent Venancio Ismael Lascano. To: Doctor Humberto Marraco, Judge. Elías Biterman, murder...*

The pilot announces he's received clearance for take-off. Eva's too relaxed in her seat, like a condemned prisoner who is resigned to her execution, just wanting everything to be over with. Nothing matters to her and she doesn't really understand why she's even on the plane, given

189

that she couldn't care less about anything. And then it happens. Just as the aircraft comes to the top of the runway, she feels it. Like a little bird fluttering its wings, like a bubble floating around in her belly. It's her child, here to remind her with this, its first perceptible movement, of the reason why she's fleeing the horror. She puts her hands on her tummy, where nervousness nestles when the plane picks up speed, where the seed grows and where she finally starts to feel that marvellous sense of fear that tells her she's alive and that she has the very best of reasons to carry on in this world. Two rows back, Doctor Fuseli, disguised as a North-American tourist, adjusts his seatbelt for take-off.

Marcelo finishes reading Lascano's report. He has analysed the evidence, the documents and the expert opinions, all with the meticulousness of a diligent student. Then, thinking that some day these documents could prove useful, he places them on a shelf in his library between two books: one, *What is Justice?* by someone called Kelsen, a gift from his father when he passed his entrance exams; the other, *A Universal History of Infamy*, a collection of short stories by Borges.

When the plane breaks through the cloud layer, which shadows the earth, and the starry sky appears, everything that's happened starts to become part of the past. The present is this kick, this child growing in her belly. This leaving behind at a thousand miles per hour the horror and the cruelty of men. She thinks, she feels, that she's inhabiting the future and that for her child's sake she'll have to heal herself, recover and rehabilitate, go back to believing that a better world is possible.

For the moment, she'd rather not know that the future is a place that only exists in the imagination.